D1490588

10 classic short stories:

One of them (*Dust Devil*) received the Shamus award from the Private Eye Writers of America.

Eight more were acclaimed in best-of-year anthologies.

The **tenth**, which is sneakily lurking in the introduction, appears here for the first time anywhere. Considering its lineage, we have high hopes for it.

Author **NANCY PICKARD** is a graduate of the University of Missouri School of Journalism.

Her first novel, *Generous Death*, introduced readers to Jenny Cain in 1983. Since then, nine more novels have appeared in the series. She has also written three novels in the Eugenia Potter series, based on the character created by Virginia Rich. Her latest series features Marie Lightfoot, a true-crime writer. Three titles are available with more to come.

Ms. Pickard is the winner of three Agatha Awards, two Macavity Awards, an American Mystery Award, two Anthony Awards, and a Shamus Award. She is a three-time Edgar nominee.

Ms. Pickard is a lifetime resident of the Kansas City area.

N A N C Y
PICKARD

STORM WARNINGS

INTERNATIONAL POLYGONICS, LTD.

New York City

STORM WARNINGS

Originally published in hardcover in 1999 by Five Star Mystery in conjunc-
tion with Tekno Books and Ed Gorman. The present publisher extends his
sincere thanks to all of these, and especially to Mr. Gorman, and assures
him that if a Mercedes were available, it would be on its way to Iowa.

Cat illustration: © copyright Christian Ivan Mejia 2002

Cover: Copyright International Polygonics, Ltd. 2002

International Polygonics, Ltd.
IPL Library of Crime Classics edition
ISBN 0-7394-2750-4

Printed and manufactured in the United States of America.

STORM WARNINGS
TABLE OF CONTENTS

SHOW & TELL

Years ago, there was a long, puzzling time when I was able to get my novels published, but not my short stories. I couldn't figure it out. What was I doing wrong in short stories that I was apparently doing right in novels? Story after story came back to me in those accursed self-addressed, stamped envelopes which we writers "send our children" out into the cold, cruel publishing world.

The idea behind SASEs, as those envelopes are not-so-affectionately known, is that when an editor turns down your story, she can stuff it right back into your own envelope and return it to you at no trouble or expense to the publisher. When I mailed my "babies" to New York City with their SASEs, I did so nervously, but also with a feeling of confidence that I had raised them right; I was sure they could get a job and fend for themselves.

But here they came back again, and again, sliding through the mail slot, looking wrinkled, exhausted and stained from their journey, falling to the floor in heaps of abject failure.

"Sorry, Mom," their accompanying rejection letters seemed to say, "There's nothing out there for us. Nobody wants us. You're the only one who loves us."

It was enough to break a mother's heart.

And then one day I attended a local writers' conference, more out of desperation than hope. For $10, I got lectures, lunch, and one piece of advice that changed my writing and my life. Another writer said that day, "Every short story needs an epiphany." Well! If an epiphany can be defined as an "Ah ha!" moment, I had one right then. I realized in a flash that's what my stories lacked, moments of meaningful revelation for a character, the reader, or both. With that advice in mind, I went home and wrote a new short story. It sold and was published. Thanks to that magical $10 piece of advice, it never slunk home looking for a rewrite—and a fresh SASE—from its mother. I'd like to show you what I mean about epiphanies, rather than just telling you, if I may. Here's a little story that I wrote while I was working on this introduction. Let's talk about it, after you read it.

It's in a Cat's Nature to Kill

"What am I going to do about you while I'm gone, Jack?"

My darling is furry and sweet. He can't help it that his nature is to kill things occasionally.

"You've brought in something dead again, haven't you, Jack?"

He closes his eyes in ecstasy as I scratch below his white whiskers.

"Now I'm going to have to go look for it, aren't I? And clean up your mess. It would be thoughtful, dear, if you'd eat all of it next time, and not leave the bits and pieces for me to pick up."

I can't help but sigh. I understand him; I don't blame Jack, but still, I sigh. I've had him for eighteen years now—he's grown old and fat on my pampering—and I am surprised he still has any hunting instinct left in him, any blood urge. Of course, he is nothing now like the hunter he used to be. In years past, in the spring when young creatures moved naively in the new grass, I sometimes came downstairs of a sunny morning to find the house littered with the detritus of his kills from the night before.

"Oh, Jack," I'd exclaimed then, knowing he couldn't help it, but feeling distressed anyway for whatever young—or old, or infirm,—at any rate, catchable—thing lay so unidentifiably scattered in raw remnants about the place. "Are these really trophies, dear, or merely leftovers?'

Even when he was kept inside, he still managed to find creatures to slaughter and even if they were vermin, their cries were hard to bear and there was still the mess to clean up afterwards. I am, by now, an expert on stain removal. Clorox and water, rug cleaner and absorbent cloths, I know which remove stains best and which stains can't be removed at all.

"Dear Jack." I stroke him as he snoozes on my lap. "So sweet and affectionate to me, and yet so merciless to defenseless creatures. How is it possible for me to love you, knowing what you do?"

I have often thought that human killers ought to be regarded as cats are. Like Jack. Both are natural born killers, born to sniff out prey, to stalk, to pounce, to tease and torture, and finally to murder and some—like Jack—to consume. But cats are coddled and adored in spite of their murderous instincts, whereas human killers are hunted down and captured, most of them. Cats are loved, as Jack is, while human killers—no less instinctual than cats, really, no more intelligent or aware or moral than a cat—are hated.

"Maybe that's the real reason certain people fear cats," I think as I gaze at my sleeping Jack. "They sense the killer inside them more than they see the loyal, dependent friend." House cats are dependent, despite what people claim about their vaunted independence. Even the most successful hunter among them still needs his care and feeding, his petting, his lap.

"Dear Jack," I murmur again, as he shifts comfortably under my hand. "You surely won't be hungry for dinner tonight." I may go ahead and set something out, but I won't go to much trouble and I won't expect him to eat it. He'll be thirsty, though. All that salt. Jack seems to drink bowls of water after a kill.

I wonder about the latest victim. For a moment, I fantasize a grieving mate and hungry babies, but then chide myself for painting a Dickensian, sentimental picture. At least it's over. I slept through it, if there was a sound. Now there is only the body—or what is left of it—to find and then the basement floor or an upstairs carpet to clean. Sometimes Jack lays his trophies nearly at my feet and other times he hides them away almost as if he were capable of feeling shame or guilt.

"No," I whisper. "Not you. I'll not invest you with emotions you are not capable of feeling. You hunt, you kill, you eat, and then it's over for you."

He is heavy on my lap.

Gently, I shift his head a bit to relieve a pinched feeling in my groin. Jack's breath clicks in his nose, but he doesn't wake.

"What am I going to do with you, Jack, while I'm away?"

This problem is also weighing heavily on me.

In all of our eighteen years together I have never left him

alone, not even for so much as one night. But my mother has died and the funeral of one's own mother is something one can't avoid. No excuses will satisfy my father or my siblings. I have to go.

But there is no way I can take Jack with me. He gets sick in cars and an airplane is out of the question.

"I'll have to ask a neighbor to look in on you."

There's a telephone on the end table to my right. I can reach it without disturbing my sleeping Jack.

"Ellen? It's Ruth, next door. I have to ask a favor. My mother died yesterday—yes, well, thank you, that's very kind of you— and I have to go to her funeral and I can't take Jack. I was wondering if you could possibly look in on him, set out some food for him? I know he's terribly spoiled and I should let him fend for himself, but he's just not used to doing that—

"You will? Oh, thank you, Ellen. I'm very grateful and I won't be gone but the one night, really, that's all I'll need."

It's all I dare.

If I leave Jack alone longer than that, poor Ellen may walk in to a scene of carnage that only I should ever have to see. Worse, Ellen herself might become the bits and pieces to which I might come home.

Prison—keeping him inside—hasn't stopped Jack.

Neutering him hasn't stopped him any more than it stops many cats.

My love and understanding haven't stopped him.

Even as he is now, white-haired and softly bearded as a Santa Claus, my darling Jack is still as true to his basic nature as a cat.

But what if something unforeseen delays me at Mother's funeral?

For a moment, I imagine vividly what I might find if I came home late. And suddenly, I realize that I must call Ellen back and cancel my request. It is one thing to enable my husband's murderous addiction by keeping it a secret and cleaning up after him. But it would be another thing entirely to lure a victim for him. That is one thing I have never done. I will not start doing it now. It is a fine distinction, perhaps, but it is my own.

x

"My poor darling." I stroke him, while thinking of the insecticide in our garage. "I'm sorry, but I have no other choice. I can't leave you alone, and I can't ask anybody to watch out for you."

Poor Jack, I am going to miss him terribly, though I'll be glad to save the carpets. Like a good cat owner with an aged and incontinent pet, I sense the time has finally come—to put him down.

§

In my first draft of that story, there was no epiphany for Ruth, no realization that she actually had a moral line, however infinitesimal, that she must not cross. There was only the slim possibility of surprising some readers with the realization that "Jack' was a man, not a cat. That wasn't enough, even assuming that anyone would be surprised, and I couldn't be sure of that. Once Ruth had her epiphany, however, the story also acquired a new irony, since not only is she about to cross an even cruder moral line by committing her own first murder, but she will use that moral line to justify it.

Epiphanies can be big or small, earnest or tongue-in-cheek, serious or comic. I think you'll find a sampling of all of those kinds in the stories that follow in this collection.

I hope you enjoy them, but then, that's their mother speaking.

—*Nancy Pickard*

Valentine's Night

Oh, yes, there really is such a thing as a blue moon.

It is an actual scientific phenomenon, caused by this and that, or something or other, but who cares about that?

That's merely science.

All that really matters is that on certain fantastical nights, some fortunate folks — who lean back on their heels and squint their eyes just so — may actually see a fabulous, delectably deep blue aura around the moon, be it full, waxing, waning, or even gibbous.

It's so strange, so beautiful, so . . . moving, somehow, that they can't stop feasting on the sight of it. They want to pluck it from the sky, to revolve it in their hands, to bring it to their nose and sniff its moonly blue fragrance, and finally to gobble it down, with blue and yellow light dribbling down their chins, as if the moon were a luscious peach bathed for that one extraordinary night in fairies' blueberry juice. It makes people greedy, a blue moon does — at least that's what some folks (not scientists) say. They claim that it makes some folks want more than they already have, more than they ever dreamed — or admitted — they'd ever need. In other words, it makes some folks crave their deepest, most secret desires. And when those desires are frustrated? Watch out! A blue moon, or so it's said, is a powerfully hungry moon, and hunger — as everybody knows — is not centered in the stomach or even the mouth, but rushes, instead, straight from the heart.

It was on such a night, the very night of Valentine's Day,

that Marianne Griff — who was normally a nice, steady, levelheaded sort of woman — figured out where her husband really was.

And it wasn't where he'd said he'd be!

No, where Ned Griff really was that night was a long way from where he had said he'd be, but only a few tempting and dangerous blocks away from home.

At six o'clock that evening, when the unwelcome knowledge tore Marianne apart like dynamite exploding in her hands, the moon had only just begun its rise in the Valentine's sky, and it wasn't even blue, not yet. Perhaps that is why Marianne was forced to endure so many hours of ordinary human misery.

"Cincinnati," was what Ned had told her. "With Christy."

Well, of course, with Christy. Marianne had easily accepted that fact. Law partners frequently traveled together. It was commonplace, wasn't it? Marianne was, herself, an account executive with a telephone company; she knew she could trust herself to travel platonically with men, so it was easy for her to trust her husband to travel innocently with women, on business.

Yes, it was true that Christy was beautiful — a shiny brunette with a body sculpted by personal trainers. Oh, and yes, Christy was youngish, with seven fewer Valentine's Days than Marianne had notched in her own belt. Oh, and brilliant, to have made full partner in her early thirties. Christy Phares was, indeed, frighteningly good at cross-examining plaintiffs' witnesses in civil courtrooms. Marianne had seen her in action, and she'd felt impressed and proud, on general feminist principles, on behalf of all women.

Get 'em, Christy! she'd thought at the time.

Christy had sat at the table on the defendant's side of the courtroom, face forward to the judge (a man), with her back straight, the palms of her hands disarmingly flat and splayed upon the table, her legs crossed at her silky knees but not at any provocative angle. In the courtroom, Christy had looked alert, sleek in her black suit, like a panther with nothing to fear in this jungle, her claws sheathed, her nostrils delicately flared, her muscles relaxed but ready to spring.

Marianne's husband, Ned, had sat at the same table, but never touched his partner, never jotted a note to her, or even lifted an eyebrow in silent dialogue. They had looked the very picture of the perfectly prepared law partners. The phrase "a matched set" had occurred to some observers, though not to Marianne. The fact that Ned was every bit as handsome and muscled and well-groomed as Christy, or that every man in the courtroom had fantasized a vision of the naked breasts beneath the black suit, was irrelevant and immaterial to Marianne. The law was all: magnificently neuter. It never occurred to Marianne — also for good feminist reasons — to suspect that Ned found less beauty in the law than he did in the lawyer seated next to him. (Even if it had just possibly crossed her mind, for one teeny second, she would have quickly shooed the treacherous thought away as being disloyal to her husband and traitorous to women.)

"We'll be at the convention hotel," he'd told her.

That made sense to Marianne; she'd doubted nothing.

But then, when she was in the bedroom changing out of her business clothes into a comfortable old gray sweatsuit, she noticed the brochure for the bar convention poking out from under some of Ned's papers that he'd left on top of the

9

chest of drawers. Curious to see who the star-spangled speakers would be this year, Marianne drew the pamphlet — *the stick of dynamite* — toward her.

The first speaker, scheduled for 8 A.M. Saturday, February eighth, was . . .

Now the dynamite was lit.

Marianne never did learn the identity of the keynote speaker for the Ohio Bar Association Convention. Her gaze had fallen back onto the date. The eighth? For a moment, she felt confused: this was Valentine's Day, February fourteenth, wasn't it?

The flame ate the wick, drawing closer to the charge.

Yes — she glanced over at the king-sized bed — there was the Valentine's card Ned had left on her pillow this morning. It was one of those modern amusing ones that were very nearly hostile in their humor, nothing sentimental or even nostalgic about it. Still, she'd been happy to receive it. He'd signed it: *"Me."* She looked into her living room and glimpsed the dozen pink carnations in a clear glass vase on her coffee table. Yes, they'd been delivered to her office today, all right, with a note: "Guess Who?"

The eighth?!

Boom.

The intuition arrived in a blast of searing pain that made Marianne feel as if she'd splashed hot grease onto her chest.

What? she thought.

And then: *No!*

To prove to herself that it wasn't true, she walked on jellied knees to the bedside telephone to dial, with trembling and suddenly freezing fingers, the convention hotel. Crazy, she thought, to feel so frightened of the phone, the very instrument she sold in such huge and profitable numbers to other people. She wished now — as it rang once, twice, in

10

Cincinnati — that it had never been invented (her own salary and profit sharing notwithstanding). The hotel operator graciously consented to look up the number and ring the room of guest Edward Griff. Marianne waited, wishing all the while that when Alexander Graham Bell had yelled, "Watson! Come here! I need you!" Watson had not replied. If only Bell had then thought, Oh, the hell with the damn thing, and given up on his invention that had changed the world. And was about to change her world. . . .

"I'm sorry, there's no Mr. Griff registered."

Marianne longed for the pony express, which would take days to reach Cincinnati and return with the terrible news of loss and heartache. At the very least, a telegraph might have taken hours.

She pleaded: "Are you sure?"

But no. Bad news came much more quickly in this century than it ever had before, giving you no time at all to arrange your emotions, your face, your voice, your future. . . .

"Yes, ma'am. Thank you for calling Marriott."

With one hand, Marianne gently hung up the telephone; with her other hand she pressed her chest, where all the pain was radiating like heat from a charcoal briquette, and she fell onto Ned's side of the bed and buried her face in his pillow. The scent of his shampoo was like a blow to her abdomen, kicking sobs up into her chest from deep inside of her. Soon she was gasping, weeping. So melodramatic, she thought, from some cynically observing part of herself. I'm dying, she thought, from another part of herself that was a good deal closer at hand, and suffering. I'll kill him! I'll kill her! I love him! I hate him! Caught painfully in a vise whose one side was steaming passion and whose other side was coolly ironic detachment, she felt exposed, absurd, primitive, raw and vulnerable and uncivilized and deeply, unfairly wounded.

For the next five and a half hours, until nearly midnight, Marianne paced the house she'd shared with a husband — a liar! — for fifteen years. Upstairs, downstairs, the basement, every room. She touched every wall and every piece of furniture, walking, walking, as if she could walk the pain off like a hangover, as if she could exhaust it out of herself, wring it out like a good sweat. She thought: It isn't true, it isn't, it is. She wept, she swore.

She took scissors and cut his Valentine's Day card into the shape of a heart, which she then cut — with jagged edges — down the middle. She taped both sides to the dresser mirror right where her face was reflected. Now she saw a broken heart surrounded by streaked blond hair with a reddened nose between the jagged edges and a forty-one-year-old neck and body below.

She panicked, she tried to meditate, she tried to read, she prayed, she screamed, she tried to reason herself back into sanity, she attempted to evolve right then and there into a better, higher sort of person, she tried to defend Ned against her own accusations, she tried to wait, to understand, to find another explanation.

She tried, she tried, she tried!

All to no effect, of course, perhaps because the moon had not yet risen to its fully royal blueness.

Finally, five minutes before the mark of midnight, the moon did appear outside her living room window.

Oh! It was fuzzy all around with a sort of incredible blue color!

Marianne stopped in her tracks, startled, staring. The sight of the moon reminded her that this day of Ned's unfaithfulness, of his wicked betrayal, was Valentine's Day.

Of all days! The schmuck!

That single awful, ironic, sentimental, full realization

struck the final shattering blow to her sadly pummeled heart. She stared at the moon — it was almost half, lying on its back in the sky like a beautiful golden fat lady in a hammock, bathed in a blue spotlight.

Marianne felt, in that moment, desperate.

She felt as if the blood inside her broken heart was spilling into the huge cavity behind her ribs, and that now the blood was lying there, helplessly pulsing at the sight of the moon, right in time to the breathing of the lady in the hammock. Marianne felt the rhythm of the moon sucking at the living pieces of her heart, tugging at her breastbone, pulling at her blood like heat drawing spilled pieces of mercury. Like an irresistible magnet, that cruel and gorgeous moon drew her out of her home and then into her car. It pulled her along the dark streets to the house where she suspected her husband lay that Valentine's night with his lover.

The golden fat lady in her hammock reached for the front fender of Marianne's car to pull her along the road to Christy's house.

This being February, there was snow everywhere.

It was cold in the car, almost immediately, when she turned the engine off, and she sat bundled in coat, hat, gloves, boots, and muffler, breathing frost into the air inside her car. There, one house down, was the two-story, red-brick house where Christy lived with her husband, Adam Phares.

A married woman!

Illuminated by the snow and the moon, the house seemed bright among the other homes on the block, as if helicopters had their spotlights beamed at it.

There! There's where the illicit couple is hiding!

13

Coupling, Marianne thought, and the word was a stab into her own side. That's where they're coupling. She looked over at her passenger's seat: God only knew why, but before she left her house she'd grabbed the vase of Ned's carnations. She'd set them on the car seat and then buckled them in, as if they were a child. It was an irrational act. So was coming here.

"But I have to have proof, don't I?" she asked the moon, plaintively.

Maybe she was being ridiculous. Oh, she liked that idea very much, and she let it warm her. Maybe she was the one who was betraying Ned, by being suspicious of him. Maybe she should be ashamed of herself for jumping to such an evil conclusion, maybe she could look forward to cringing with secret humiliation whenever she looked back on this awful night. Oh, yes! She'd happily trade that little private mortification for the more public one she'd been imagining: being left for a younger woman. So banal; could it possibly be worth all this heartache?

The earth swung in its orbit, passing the moon behind a cloud, then out again on the other side. Perfidious, nomadic moon! Silently, it seemed to swing into Marianne's vision, its blue halo catching the corner of her eye, snagging her attention so that she turned her head, the exact forty-five degrees that was needed to direct her attention to . . .

Ned's car.

It was parked across the street from Christy's house in the parking lot of a condominium complex, sneaked in between a red BMW and a vintage Mustang, as if it belonged there. Maybe it wasn't his. There were nearly as many Mercedes in the city as there were lawyers. Maybe. But no, the light of the snow from below lit the personalized license: L EAGLE (short for legal eagle). And the moon shone reveal-

14

ingly on the dark (sinister) gray finish of the car.

No mistake: it was Ned's incriminating car.

The moon looked bluest at that very moment when Marianne's heart pulsed so hard she thought surely it would jerk from her chest and hop down the snowy street without her, plop by bloody plop.

"Oh, God," she groaned, mostly from the pain of finding out she was right, but also from the problem of trying to use a tissue to wipe her nose while she still had gloves on. The worst of her pain was centered just inside the warm tender curve of her left breast. She pressed her fingers there, and leaned into them. *Oh* . . .

The unrelenting moon pulled Marianne's hand away from her wounded breast — like a shot bird, she was — and placed the fingers on the handle of the car door, which opened. The moon tugged her out into the street and pushed her hands to close the door with a muted *click*. It shoved her hands into the pockets of her overcoat and pulled the breath from her mouth in a white mist. It made her stand alone under a street lamp for a moment, staring helplessly, furiously, at Christy's house.

And then the moon — the plump, soft invisible tugging hand of the fat lady in the hammock — touched Marianne's chin and nudged it to the left, drawing her attention to another car.

This one — an ivory Infiniti — was parked at the curb.

She saw a man seated in it, and he was also staring at Christy's house.

The moon caught his chin and turned it toward her.

It was Christy's husband, Adam Phares.

Simultaneously, he and Marianne gasped, and then flushed with the embarrassment of being caught in the act of having their hearts broken. And then the moon, merciless

15

creature, placed its fat blue hands on the woolly lapels of Marianne's coat and jerked her right into the passenger seat of Adam's car.

"I'll kill the son of a bitch," were his first words to her.

"Just Ned?" she retorted, in a shaky voice. "What about your wife? Where did she tell you she'd be this weekend?"

"I told her I'd be in New York."

Marianne thought about that, and then exclaimed: "You *knew?*"

"I was only suspicious. *Now* I know."

"How long do you think it's been going on?"

He shook his head. "What difference does it make if it's more than one night?"

Marianne slumped down in the seat. "It doesn't." Wearily, feeling defeated, she turned her head toward him. "So what are you going to do?"

"Make sure," he said, lingering over each word, nailing them into the night. "You want to come with me?"

"Where?" And when he nodded in the direction of the house, she exclaimed: "Over there? You're kidding!"

"It's my house —" He looked distracted. "I'm sorry, I can't remember your name."

"Marianne."

"I'm Adam."

She knew that, but they'd only met at office parties. She couldn't remember what he did for a living, she didn't know anything about him, except that apparently his wife was cuckolding him with Marianne's husband.

"Marianne," he repeated. "It's my house. I can do anything I want to."

"But what —"

"I want to see them together."

He picked up a thirty-five-millimeter camera from the

16

console between them and held it up. "*Catch* them together."

"Oh, my God, are you sure —"

"They're *lawyers,* Marianne."

"Right." She nodded, immediately grasping the harrowing prospect of divorcing an attorney. "Okay, then I'm coming, too." As he stuck the little camera into the right-hand pocket of his overcoat, an even more frightening idea occurred to her. "But what if they hear us and think we're burglars and call the police? Do you keep guns in the house? What if they mistake us for burglars and shoot us?"

"So they call the cops, so what?" Adam Phares tightened his lips, as if to draw them in from the cold. "So they shoot us." He added, angrily, dully, "So what?"

Then they'd be sorry, Marianne thought, before she corrected herself. No, they wouldn't. She bit her lips to restrain the sob that wanted to burst from her mouth.

The moon, having done its mischievous job, ducked behind a cloud and wisely stayed there.

"Can't you sneak more quietly?" she hissed, behind Adam, as they approached the bushes in front of the back bedroom window. She'd hoped the snow would muffle their approach, but no, the ice crunched like peanut brittle. Plus, Adam seemed intent on bulling his way like a defensive end charging a quarterback: his arms swinging wide of his coat, his head jutted out ahead of his body, his boots taking giant strides, he seemed oblivious of the noise he was making. She felt as if they were alerting the neighborhood, much less the lovers. "Adam, wait!"

She ran, crunchingly, after him, catching him by his coattails and jerking him back toward her. "We'll never

17

catch them if they hear us coming first!"

It was reassuring to her that he was behaving as irrationally as she felt that she was.

They covered the rest of the distance like cautious rabbits in the snow. Adam led Marianne smack up against a windowsill toward the rear of the house, and they stood side by side, peering in, standing on top of dead and frozen marigold plants.

The lovers hadn't bothered to close the curtains.

They'd even thoughtfully left a light on in a bathroom, and that, plus the light from the moon and the snow, illuminated them like lovers on the cover of a book.

Marianne stared at the tumble of blankets on the huge bed inside.

At first, she couldn't make out any human forms, but then a fold in the white sheets revealed itself to be a slim and shapely female arm, pale and crooked at the elbow so that the forearm lay on top of a larger pile of blankets that revealed themselves to be a curve of male chest and shoulders. Finally, Marianne could make out the tousle of two dark heads in the shadows of the pillows, two heads sleeping so close together they looked like one, a giant's.

The giant on the bed didn't stir.

"Must be exhausted," Marianne muttered, spitefully.

"What?" Adam whispered.

She didn't answer, but pointed, instead, at something inside.

"What?" he asked again.

"The mirror," she told him.

There was a mirrored double closet door directly to the side of the sleeping lovers and directly across from their spouses standing outside the window in the snow. Marianne and Adam could look in the mirror at themselves looking in

18

at Christy and Ned. Marianne moved her own head slightly, to superimpose it on top of Christy's head: now it was she who was sleeping beside her husband. Feeling reckless, Marianne turned her face and puckered her lips: her image seemed to kiss the man on the bed.

"What are you doing?" Adam hissed, and when she shifted her glance from the mirror to him, she discovered that her lips were pointed in his direction.

"Embarrassing myself," she said.

Suddenly he put his left arm around her shoulders in a strong, abrupt motion that let her know he was trying to comfort her. "I'm sorry," he said.

"Me, too," she whimpered, and she tucked her right hand into the left pocket of his overcoat. "They look . . . happy."

"Wonderful."

She laughed a little at his sarcastic tone, but she couldn't stop staring at the bed, and neither, it appeared, could Adam. Maybe it wasn't so much that Christy and Ned looked happy — Marianne couldn't, after all, even see their faces — but that they looked warm, cozy, loving. Those adjectives added up to happiness in Marianne's personal dictionary. She and Ned hadn't slept entwined like that since before they were married, not unless one of them was a little drunk. Even after they made love, there were only a few brief moments of embracing, then a quick, rather astringent kiss, and then they turned their backs to one another, each moving to opposite sides of their bed to sleep. But Marianne knew what Christy would be feeling — if she were awake — with Ned's arm underneath her head, how big and masculine and firm Ned's upper arm and shoulder would feel, and how much heat his body would be giving off. Marianne imagined she could feel some of that heat radiating all the way outside, melting some of the snow where she was standing.

Suddenly, Adam raised his right hand and touched his glove to the storm window. Snow that had been stuck to his glove filtered down to their boots. His fingers were splayed against the glass. It was a hurt and forlorn gesture that made Marianne's heart ache for him. She pulled her hand out of his pocket and snaked her arm around to his back and patted him two or three times as if to say, "There, there."

After a moment, she had to admit to him, "My feet are freezing."

"Okay, come on." He grabbed her right hand in his left and pulled her away from the window. Together, like linked burglars, they made their way the rest of the distance around to the back of the house.

Adam used his key to open two locks almost without any noise.

Marianne held her breath as he pushed open the door.

"We'll track snow," she warned.

"It'll melt. They'll think they did it."

She entered the darkened kitchen of her husband's lover, stepping right behind her husband's lover's husband.

There was only a light on the stove and the brightness of the night outside, but once their eyes adjusted, they could see perfectly well.

"Take your coat?" Adam asked her.

She almost smiled as she took it off and handed it to him. Christy's husband had nice hospitable instincts, even under pressure. Removing her coat seemed to Marianne to be the most daring thing she'd done so far, because it might keep her from making a clean, fast getaway. She felt as if she'd taken the big step off the high cliff.

"Boots?" he asked, looking undecided.

Boldly, she nodded, and they both removed their boots and then lined them up facing the door, as if they could jump into them in a second, like the Lone Ranger onto the back of Silver. Marianne even took off her hat and unwound her muffler and put it all, including her gloves, on top of her coat, which he'd placed on a high stool.

They looked around the kitchen, which was messy with the signs of a dinner having been recently prepared and nothing cleaned up or put away.

"She never cooks for me anymore," Adam complained.

"He never did cook for me," Marianne retorted.

It appeared that the happy couple had fixed a Valentine's dinner together, and a good one: pasta still clung to the edges of a big silver pot, and you could see where butter and bits of parsley and other goodies had been stirred in a sautéeing pan. The oven door had been left wide open, and it revealed a greasy broiling pan with a butcher knife and a sliver of steak fat still on it.

The smell of garlic permeated the air.

Adam lifted a dried string of pasta from the pot and nibbled morosely on it, while Marianne walked to a doorway and looked into the next room, which turned out to be a dining room. She crooked her finger at Adam, who came over to stand beside her. Together, they gazed in at a dining room table set elegantly for two: white china with gold bands on it, heavy silver service, candles galore, and a silver decanting rack for the red wine.

"She'll be sorry," Adam said, sounding gruff and satisfied. When Marianne gave him a quizzical look, he explained: "Christine can't tolerate red wine. Gives her migraines."

Marianne said: "I hope she throws up."

"She will, you can count on it."

"Good. Any chance it'll kill her?"

"Probably not," he said glumly, and walked back into the kitchen. He opened the refrigerator. Marianne watched him remove an orange-and-black carton and take a clean glass from a cupboard, then pour orange juice into it. He then bent over and opened the cabinet doors under the sink and began to remove various cans and bottles.

Curious, Marianne went over to watch what he was doing.

Adam took a bottle of window cleaner and sprayed some of the contents into the orange juice. He looked at Marianne. "She drinks a glass of orange juice whenever she has a hangover. I've tried to tell her that tomato juice is more effective, but she always knows better." He set the window cleaner down and picked up a can of abrasive bathroom cleanser and shook some of it into the juice.

"Won't she taste it?" Marianne asked, feeling oddly detached.

"She'll think it's the hangover."

Marianne reached around him to pick up a plastic bottle that contained ammonia, and she poured a dollop of that into the orange brew.

"You'd think it'd bubble or something," she said.

He grunted. "It will, inside her."

Marianne laughed, and then he did, too. When they had emptied a little of everything into their witch's potion, he carefully poured it all back into the orange juice carton, and then he washed out the glass and put it into the dishwasher.

"Now it'll be diluted," Marianne said, feeling disappointed.

"No, there's not much left in the carton," Adam assured

her as he returned it to the refrigerator. They looked at each other and smiled, and then they turned to appraise the contents of the kitchen again. Adam seemed to be drawn to the huge butcher knife lying sideways across the meat broiler. He slid it out of the oven and held it up in the air so that for a moment he looked to Marianne like a medieval warrior.

He glanced over at her. "What'd you think?"

She shook her head. "No, you'd be sure to get caught."

"You think?" He walked over to where there was a butcher-block table, and without warning, he violently plunged the knife into the wood, groaning with his effort. Then he backed away, and he and Marianne watched the handle of the knife quiver in the odd light in the night kitchen. She had gasped when he did it, but now she was mesmerized by how deeply the knife had penetrated the table.

Adam broke the charged silence. "Is he a good lover?"

Marianne shrugged. "If you love him."

He stared at her. "Don't you?"

"Don't I what?"

"Love him?"

"After tonight? How could I!"

"It's been done before," he said wryly. "I'm more interested in before tonight. Did you love him before tonight?"

"I thought I did. Now I don't know. Do you love her?"

Adam grasped the still-moving knife handle and tried to pull it out. It wouldn't come loose. "What's love got to do with it?" he said, and then gestured to her. "Come on."

In the dining room, Adam looked at the table and said, "Somebody's been sitting in my chair."

"And eating your porridge."

They didn't have to say the next line out loud: "And sleeping in your bed."

There was an opened gift box of designer chocolates on the table, with several pieces missing. And there were a dozen perfect pink roses in a chic black vase. And there were two Valentine's Day cards lying on the table.

Marianne took a piece of chocolate, stuck it in her mouth, and picked up the cards to read. They were as sentimental as the one that Ned had given her was not; they were as gooey as the chocolate. The handwritten extra message on one of them, in the handwriting that wasn't Ned's, said: "Darling, I love you more than life itself." Marianne handed that card to Adam, who read it and then said: "Let's find out if she means it."

Marianne felt a sudden chill of coldness, a splash of jarring reality. She swallowed the chocolate, which felt like a marble going down. This was no game they were playing. Poisoned orange juice in the refrigerator. Butcher knife in the table. With her heart trip-hammering, she watched as Adam disappeared back into the kitchen. When he returned, there was a lump in his suit coat pocket — unlike her, he hadn't changed out of his work clothes — that he was patting with his hand.

"Adam," she said, weakly. "I don't —"

She didn't what? She didn't know.

"Come on," he said, and she followed him, like a puppy being trained. On her way out of the dining room, she picked up a couple more pieces of the chocolate.

It was easy to follow the clues to the next stage in the illicit couple's evening: a trail of discarded clothing started at the beginning of a hallway and led to an open door. Marianne and Adam found, in order: a woman's belt, man's belt, woman's blouse, man's shirt, woman's skirt, woman's shoes, hose, garter belt, black bra, black panties, and finally, a man's trousers. At the last item, Marianne knelt down.

She pulled Ned's wallet from his right rear trouser pocket and removed from it the photograph of herself and the one of them together.

Adam tapped her shoulder.

When she looked up, she saw that he was holding down to her his own wallet-sized photograph of Christy. Marianne slipped it into one of the empty slots in her husband's wallet. She also pulled out all the cash and then emptied his front pockets of change.

She held the money up to Adam, offering him some, or all.

He took the bills, went back to his wife's hosiery, and stuck the money down inside one of the legs.

Nasty, Marianne thought, and smiled to herself. She put the change back in his pocket, for lack of any better — or quieter — idea of what to do with it. Now Ned might suspect that his lover had stolen his money and even had the nerve to substitute her own photo for his family pictures. He wouldn't like that, the overconfidence of it, even if he decided, as he would, that it was only a joke. And *she* really wouldn't like his idea of humor: sticking cash in her stockings, as if she were some hooker. And they could each deny it until their faces were as blue as the moon, but who else could have done it, as they were all alone in the house at the time!

As an extra fillip, Marianne stuck the two chocolates deep in the left rear pocket of Ned's trousers.

There!

She smiled up at Adam, feeling almost satisfied now.

But he was staring into the bedroom beyond her, ignoring her childlike pleasure in their petty vengeance. And he was reaching toward the right-hand pocket of his suit coat.

As he walked past her, Marianne grabbed at his coat, frantically, but it only served to pull her off balance, so that she had to scramble to keep from crashing onto the floor of the hallway. For a panicked instant, she wondered if that would have been best: maybe she should scream, warn them. . . .

Adam stepped to the door of the bedroom, and pulled out his camera.

Marianne sank against a wall in relief so flooding she thought: This must be how pregnant women feel when their water breaks. Oh, God, she'd thought it was a gun. She tiptoed to a bathroom down the hall and used it. When she returned, Adam was still standing in the doorway, the camera at his side. She took her place beside him, his companion voyeur.

There they were, sprawled, blanket coated, sleeping off the booze and lust. (Marianne refused to call it love.)

Adam leaned over and spoke right into her ear. His breath tickled her as he said: "Your husband's better looking than I am."

Into his ear, Marianne responded: "She's better looking than I am." (Particularly now, Marianne thought, knowing how red her nose and eyes must be, after the cold and so much crying.)

He leaned over again. "Yeah, but we're much nicer."

She hadn't expected that, and muffled a snort of laughter behind her hands. When she looked at him again, he was smiling at her, but his brown eyes were glistening. For the first time, she really saw him: an attractive man, possibly a little younger than she, with a broad forehead and a long, slim nose and nice eyes. It was true, he wasn't as handsome as Ned was. And she wondered if the other was true: was he really any nicer?

"I'm so tired," she confessed.

He nodded and took her hand and led her down the hall.

Silently, in total understanding, they both lay down — fully clothed — on the white chenille cover on the double bed in the guest bedroom down the hall. They held hands, each of them staring at the ceiling.

"Did you get the pictures?"

"Yeah."

"Good. I guess."

Just as she was starting to go to sleep, he said, "She's not really prettier than you are. She's just smoother. It's like she licks herself down every night, like a cat." He sounded so serious, Marianne thought, as he said these awful things about his wife. "When she sees herself in a mirror, she nearly purrs."

To keep it even, Marianne said, "He's all clothes and haircut."

Adam turned his head on his pillow, toward Marianne. "Your face is much more interesting than hers ever will be. Yours isn't just pretty, it also has character."

"After tonight it sure will."

Her tone was sarcastic, but he'd made her feel a little better.

He was almost asleep when Marianne said: "Is she your best friend?"

"I guess not."

They both fell asleep, feeling comforted by the hand they held.

In the morning, they awoke to the unmistakable sounds of their spouses making love to one another in the next room. At first, Marianne thought she would weep with the terrible sorrow and longing she experienced. But when

Adam pounded his fist into the mattress, Marianne felt sheer fury. Finally, they found themselves laughing at the moaning, the groaning, at the "Oh, God"s and the "Oh, Yes"es, until they were helplessly clinging to each other, stifling each other's hysteria.

And then they heard their spouses get up from the bed. Gather their clothes, get dressed.

"Is this your idea of a joke?" demanded Christy, from the hall.

"I didn't do that!" Ned protested. "I'd never do that."

"Well, who the hell did? Nobody else has been here! Jesus, I can't believe you'd insult me like this!"

"Christy!"

"Damn, don't yell at me, I have a migraine."

In the other bedroom, Marianne clutched Adam and whispered in horror: "Oh, my God!"

He sat up, and she saw the wild look on his face.

"Try orange juice," they heard Ned say.

"No. Adam always says that tomato juice is best."

"Oh, well, if Adam says it —"

"I believe I can make my own decision about what to do for my own hangover," was Christy's cold response to that.

Adam lay back down, grinning.

"But our coats!" Marianne hissed at him. "Our boots!"

He pointed to a chair, where Marianne saw all their belongings piled up, and he whispered back: "I woke up in the middle of the night and brought it all in here."

"What woke you?"

"The sound of Christy throwing up in the bathroom."

Marianne buried her face in the sleeve of his suit coat and grinned, despite the tears in the corners of her eyes.

The edgy, angry voices of the lovers moved out of the hall, into the dining room.

But in a few minutes, Christy's voice was coming back at them, saying, ". . . just get it the hell out of my chopping block! What do you expect me to believe, that I walked in my sleep and stuck it there? Honest to God, Edward, I never dreamed you'd have this childish kind of practical-joke humor. I have to tell you that I am *not* amused . . ."

And her footsteps sounded in the master bedroom, followed by the sounds of slamming drawers and doors.

From the vicinity of the front door, Ned called out: "Do you want to ride with me, Christy?"

"No!" she called back. "I'll drive my own car!"

"I love you!" he yelled, angrily, at her.

"Love you, too!" she yelled back, sounding furious. And then they followed that with loud good-byes, and he slammed the front door behind him.

"Ass!" Christy said, in the next room.

She slammed her way out the back door shortly after that.

It was Marianne's turn to shoot up in bed.

"Oh, my God," she said. "Our cars are outside."

But Adam was starting to laugh again. He pulled her back down on the bed. "That's okay. She'll steam out of the driveway so fast, she'll never see mine. And he'll never think that out of all of the gray Accords in the world, that one could possibly be yours."

Marianne turned toward him. "Should we feel sorry for them?"

He thought about that. "I guess we can afford to be charitable."

They gazed at each other, and then said, at exactly the same time: "Nah." They burst out laughing in a fit that continued until Marianne fell into one last crying jag. Adam held her sympathetically, tactfully, until it ended. Then they got up, gathered their belongings, straightened themselves up, and left the house by the front door.

Before they left, however, Adam gathered up the dozen beautiful pink roses and swept them into his arms, making a lovely, if dripping, bundle of them. He presented them, with a gallant bow, to Marianne.

"Will you be my Valentine?" he asked her.

She took the flowers and cradled them. Feeling suddenly shy, she said to him, "Well, maybe next year."

Adam Phares waved his camera at her as he drove off.

Marianne waved the roses at him. Then she took the carnations, opened her car door, and dumped them in the slushy street. She placed the roses carefully in the vase, made sure it was still securely buckled in, and headed home.

Behind her, the moon, nearly invisible now, looked pale and ordinary in the morning sky. The fat lady was gone. Nobody, seeing it right then, would have guessed it had ever been blue.

A Rock and a Hard Place

I'm not a hard woman; I'm only a private investigator.

You see me, you think I'm an athlete, a tough girl, even at my age, which is fifty-one. You hear my voice, my language sometimes, you think, she's a rough one. But I'm college educated, with two degrees, one of them in English lit, believe it or not. Besides, lifting weights never built up muscles between a person's ears, if you see what I mean. I work out on computers more than I do at the gym, that's the nature of this job.

It's fairly respectable, my profession.

I'm fairly respectable, is what I'm saying, even if I do carry weapons and use them, even if I did serve in Vietnam for six months that are supposed to be top secret, even now, and even if I have witnessed sordid scenes and participated in violent acts. I still maintain I am basically a respectable and mostly law-abiding person, or I was, until recently. Now, I don't know what I am. Except that one thing I am for sure is dying. Yeah, right, aren't we all? No, I mean, specifically me, specifically now, from breast cancer. My doctors claim they excised it with one of those "partials," but I don't believe them. I hear it growing, infinitesimal and stealthy, escaping their means of detection, but not mine. The saving grace is: I'm good at guns. Things get bad, too painful, I always have my stockpile of large and little friends, the ones with the long noses and the short ones, the loud voices and the soft. Dying definitely does not scare me; I would not move one foot off the sidewalk to get out of its way.

Are we clear on all this, so far?

I was already all of those things I have just described — except the part about not knowing any longer what I am — at the moment when Grace Kairn (not her real name) applied her knuckles to a tentative knock on my office door. I looked up from my Macintosh Quadra, where I was trying to hack my way into a database I wasn't supposed to be able to get into, and saw her: late thirties, really short blond hair, Audrey Hepburn bones, one of those women who makes a woman like me feel big and bulky and clumsy, like we're all muscle and cuss words and she's all lace and fragrance.

"Hello?" she said, from my doorway. "Angela Fopeano?"

Immediately, I was awkward, not at my best, barking back at her like I was an MP and she was a private caught off base.

"Yeah!" I said.

Yeah. As if my mother hadn't raised me to say "yes," or to be polite, to be a nice girl. *Yeah. Duh. I'm Angie.*

"Who are you?" I asked her, point-blank, like that.

God, sometimes I make myself cringe.

"I'm Grace Kairn, may I talk to you, do you have time?"

No appointment. I hate that. Who do people think they are, expecting me to drop everything for them? I always do, though, because one of my failings is curiosity. God knows, I would hesitate to call it intellectual. Still, I want to *know*, even when I'm pissed at people — who they are, what they want. People in general were starting to bore me, though, with their repetitive stories about infidelity and fraud and deception and greed. Big deal. Did they think that made them different? It was all starting to feel banal and sordid. My own clients were beginning to bore me. Bad sign for a working gal. What did I think I was going to do if I didn't solve crimes? *Crimes,* hah. Misdemeanors of the ego, was more like it, that was what I investigated. Who was sleeping with whom. Who cooked the books. Who stole the paper clips. Who the hell cared. Not me anymore.

Man, I sound angry, don't I? Even I can hear it.

At least this woman asked if I had the time.

I waved her into a chair, and she looked across my desk at me with the gentlest smile I ever saw in anybody's blue eyes. In a humble kind of way, definitely not boasting, she said, "What I have to say is . . . maybe . . . unusual."

"Uh huh."

Yeah right, I thought, tell me a new one, or better yet give me a cure for cancer.

"I want to hire you," she said concisely, gently, "to prevent three murders."

"You have my attention," I said, wryly. "I'm taping this."

"All right." Her voice was a sweet, melodic breeze across my desk, and I couldn't imagine she could have anything so very "unusual" to tell me. In fact, her first words were ordinary, to my jaded ears. "Five years ago, before Christmas of that year, I was held up at gunpoint in a parking lot of the Oberlin South Mall."

She was surprisingly direct, for someone so soft.

I sat back and listened.

"It was one man, with a gun, and he pushed me into the car and made me drive him out of town to a riverbank. And he raped me and shot me and left me there, thinking I was dead."

Jesus, I thought, and was surprised to feel tears in my eyes.

I cleared my throat. "I guess you weren't dead."

"No." She smiled, a wonderful, calming, gentle expression of serenity that I instantly coveted. "I *was* dead."

"Okay."

"To be specific, I was still alive when he left me, but I was bleeding to death and I was in shock and I was starting to be hypothermic, it was winter, after all, and I was lying in the snow."

Dear God, I thought. I hated this story already, and I didn't want to hear any more of it, but at least it had a happy ending. Didn't it? I mean, she was there, telling me her terrible tale, wasn't she?

Raped. Shot. Lying in snow.

I stared at the gentle, delicate woman seated across from me, and tried very hard *not* to allow a picture of the warlike scene to come into my mind.

Sweet Mother Mary.

And I'm not even Catholic.

"I was still alive when the paramedics arrived," Grace Kairn told me, while my stomach knotted as she spoke, "because a passing driver with a phone in his car found me pretty quickly. But I died in the ambulance on the way back into town. I was dead for ten minutes. No heartbeat. No brain activity. No respiration. They said I was absolutely, clinically dead."

"Yeah? One of those near-death experiences?"

I sat up, interested for obvious reasons. It's always good to meet a tourist who has already visited your next destination. They can clue you in as to the weather, what to wear. I'd heard plenty of those tales in 'Nam, but that was a long time ago, and these days I have a more personal interest in collecting any available data. As she told the familiar tale of the tunnel, the light, the love at the end of it, her face was — aren't they all — glowing with happiness. She almost, but not quite, made me want some of it.

But I was still waiting to hear anything "unusual."

"While I was dead," Grace Kairn said, predictably, "I felt

34

loved in a way that I can never fully describe to anyone who hasn't felt it. And I learned some things from that love . . ."

I couldn't help it, I had to ask: "Like, what?"

She smiled, almost a grin, catching me in my curiosity. Before she could reply, I realized we'd better skip the fantasies and cut to the chase. "So who do you want me to keep from getting killed?" I asked her.

But she would tell it at her pace, not mine.

"The man who attacked me was captured and tried and convicted of armed robbery and put into prison."

"Just armed robbery? Was it a plea bargain?"

"Yes. He served four years of his sentence."

"Four . . . you mean he's out now?"

"Yes," she said, gently, "he is."

I felt a chill for her sake.

At that moment, I also experienced a strange, physical sense of a compression of time; it seemed to cast my office in shadow, as if the day were drawing too quickly to a close. All in all, I had a sudden and unaccountable feeling of urgency, which I tried to quell within me, because it was weirdly close to panic.

I couldn't remember the last time I'd felt panic.

"And you're afraid?" I asked her.

Or was I talking to myself?

She glanced out my window, smiling a little to herself, before she looked back at me. "I'll tell you the truth, the answer to that is yes and no. I'm not afraid of anything for myself, certainly not of dying, not anymore. But yes, I'm . . . afraid . . . for other people."

"Who?"

"My husband." The expression in her eyes made me envy any person who occasioned such affection. "Rick absolutely believes that I really died. In Rick's eyes, the man who

. . . killed me . . . is a murderer. Not an attempted murderer. A *murderer* who should have been convicted of premeditated homicide."

"But you're alive," I pointed out.

"But I was dead," she countered, quite firmly. "He did kill me."

I let out a whistle. "Try telling that to the law."

"We did — to the police, to the prosecutors, to the judge, to the jury, to anybody who would listen, but they laughed at us. Not openly, they weren't that unkind, but they didn't take us seriously, because, as you yourself said . . ." Grace Kairn touched her blouse above her heart. "I'm alive." Then she added the kicker: "Rick says he'll kill the man who murdered me."

"Murdered you."

"I was dead."

"And you want me to keep Rick from doing that?"

"Oh, yes!"

"You want me to protect the man who assaulted you?"

I heard my own voice rise in disbelief and protest at the idea of it, and yet, I understood the logic of her plea: She didn't want her husband to commit a murder — a real one — and go to jail for it. And he would, because — trust me — the law *is* an ass, and so are many of the men and women who administer it. It wouldn't matter that he killed a very bad guy, or that he was acting out of perfectly understandable rage at the man and the system. He'd still get the very sentence the true bad guy didn't get. Grace Kairn was correct to fear for her husband. Not to mention the fact that he could, instead, get himself killed by the bad guy, and then what would become of *her*, left alone in the universe with a monster?

Her thoughts were way ahead of mine. "Yes," she affirmed, "I want you to protect that man and I also want you to protect Rick, so he doesn't get himself killed."

"Who's the third person?" I asked her.

She had said she wanted me to prevent three murders.

"Well, it's me." She smiled that gentle smile. "The man who killed me — his name is Jerry Heckler — has friends who have sent me threatening letters and phone calls, all of them saying that Heckler will 'get me' when he gets out." She blushed at the phrase, "get me," as if she were embarrassed to be uttering such a cliché, but that's about as disturbed as she seemed to be. The fact that this vicious bastard — this Jerry Heckler (also not his real name) — was once again free to hurt her seemed not to perturb her peace of mind. I, on the other hand, felt a quickening of horror on her behalf and a heavy dose of rage. I utterly sympathized with her husband's vendetta. Like I always say, where's the goddamned death penalty when you really need it?

"Okay," I said, "so you want me to protect Jerry Heckler so your husband won't do something stupid and get arrested for it. And you want me to protect Rick, so Heckler doesn't kill him for trying. And you want me to protect you, so Heckler can't kill you. Again."

"No," she said, gently correcting me. "I want you to protect all of us, because killing is . . . wrong. Under any circumstances, for any reason, it's a . . . mistake." That weird look of serenity — the one I coveted — came over her face again. "That's one of the things I learned."

"Just a mistake?"

"An error."

"Mistakes can be corrected," I pointed out. "But if I kill somebody, he's never coming back."

She smiled at me. "I'm back."

I agreed to take the case. Not for her reason. I didn't believe her reason. I accepted her advance money for *my* reason: That bastard Heckler was not going to hurt this nice woman again — or any other woman — if I could prevent it, and he was also not going to lure her husband into making a stupid, possibly fatal mistake.

"Will you agree to do what I tell you?" I asked her, and then when she said she would, I asked her to give me a few minutes to think about what that was going to be.

Because I felt such urgency for her sake, I sent Grace Kairn immediately out of town to stay with my mother, figuring Heckler would never know to look there. I didn't even let her go home to pack. I told her not even to call home until I okayed it; I'd inform and deal with her husband — that was part of what she was paying me for.

Maybe you think I was wrong to take a chance on endangering my own mother, but then you've never met Mom. Her only child grew up to be in the military, and then became a private investigator. Think about it: This is probably a mother who can take care of herself. Anyway, who do you think first taught me to shoot? Not Dad, he'd have been the one she shot if he'd ever come back to the rotten neighborhood he left us in. She'd have told the cops she thought he was a prowler, and I'd have backed up her story, even while I was privately thinking, is this any kind of woman for a man to marry? My mother cracks me up; I think she's great, but I can see how she looks from Dad's point of view.

Anyway, once I had Grace safe, the next three steps on my list were: visits, of varying degrees of cordiality, to Rick Kairn, Lt. Janet Randolph, and Mr. Jerry Heckler.

In descending order of cordiality, I started with the cop.

"On a scale of clear water to cesspool, Janet," I said to

her in her office, "where does this Heckler fall?"

"Close your mouth *and* hold your nose."

"That bad?"

"You can't be too careful with this one, Angie." The lieutenant, no beauty queen to begin with, hiked an eyebrow,
which gave her the appearance of a quizzical rottweiler:
black hair, brown skin, pugnacious face, aggressive nature.
"What *are* you going to do?"

"Take a look at him."

"That's all?"

I grinned at her. "Somebody's got to be able to identify
the body."

Her answering smile was grim. "We were all hoping
some other prisoner would kill him."

"It's not too late for that. The world is full of
ex-prisoners."

"Don't I know it."

"Can I see a picture of him?"

"You don't need to. He's not real hard to spot. He's a
carrottop."

I had to laugh. "You're kidding."

"No. If I had carrot hair, I would never be a criminal.
Criminals are so stupid."

"He's out after only four years. So who's stupid? Him or
us?"

She handed me the address of the halfway house where
he was residing. I wanted to say, "Good dog." Janet had
been in Vietnam, too, but in spite of the fact that we were
coffee friends, she didn't know I had been there, and there
was no way she could look it up, because those files don't
exist. Hardly anybody now living does know. It's not too difficult, pretending innocence. People don't expect a woman
veteran, not even other women. When Janet or some other

39

'Nam vet starts in on their war stories or trauma tales, I know how to widen my eyes and look awed and sympathetic.

She doesn't know about the cancer, either.

I'm good at disguise, so I went home and put one together.

I put on my black wig that is long enough to make a ponytail and that has bangs down to my eyelashes . . . and I put in my false bridgework that gives me an overbite . . . and my green contacts and plain glasses . . . and from out of my Goodwill clothing pile I selected a soiled white waitress uniform and dirty white waitress shoes. But my best trick is probably the only one I ever really need: I increased my bust size dramatically enough to draw a man's eyes away from my face. I added makeup, which I usually don't wear, or dangly earrings, either, and I offered a silent apology to all of the legitimate, hardworking waitresses in the world.

One good thing about a DD cup is that you can snug a pistol right down in there between the pads, and nobody suspects a thing unless they try to hug you. If you ever see a buxom waitress reaching in to adjust her bra strap — duck.

Thus camouflaged, I set off to find Jerry Heckler.

Do not assume I took that visit lightly.

There's a writer, Andrew Vachss, who wrote a short story I read one time that I'll never forget, because he was so right. In the story, which was called "The White Crocodile," Vachss compares certain kinds of people to crocodiles. He says baby crocodiles get abandoned by their mothers, so they have to fend for themselves, and if they live to be adults, they spend the rest of their lives getting even.

I figured Jerry Heckler was one of the world's crocodiles.

It didn't matter how much theoretical pity I might feel for whatever abuse he might have suffered as a child, the fact remained he was a man now and he would rend other people limb from limb and eat them if they got within striking distance of him, as proved by what he did to Grace Kairn.

I don't mess around with the Jerry Hecklers of the world; there's no talking to them, no reasoning with them, no sympathy to be got from them, they have no conscience, they are the most dangerous kind of human being that exists, the crocodiles of the human kingdom, and they have — quoting Vachss again — no natural enemies. If I have to deal with them at all, I do the only thing you can do, what I was taught first by my mother and then in 'Nam: strike first.

I made him within half an hour of waiting at a bus stop across from the halfway house. Suppertime. Carrottop came out of the halfway house and walked two doors down to a deli.

While he ate, I made use of the time by getting on the pay phone across the street and calling Grace Kairn's husband, Rick. There was no need for me to go see him personally, not when I had only one basic message to deliver, which was: Don't do it, you'll get caught. According to the schedule Grace had given me, her husband should be home from work now, and only just beginning to wonder where his wife could be.

"Rick? My name is Angela Fopeano, and I'm a private investigator that your wife hired today. She wants me to keep you from trying to kill Jerry Heckler."

I couldn't mince words; Heckler might eat fast.

Kairn was incoherent, indignant, frightened, on the other end of the line, but I could tell he really did love his wife, because he verbally took his frustrations out on me, not on her at what she'd done that day to knock his pins out from under him.

I interrupted Kairn to tell him, "Here's how I'm going to stop you from making a dead man or a prisoner out of yourself, Rick. I have been to see Lt. Janet Randolph today and I have informed her of your intention to kill Heckler."

Dead silence from Kairn.

So often the simple way is the best way.

There was nothing he could do now, without getting himself — and by extension, his wife — in a hell of a mess. And if he loved her — which she believed, and I did too — he just wouldn't do that. It was one thing for him to rant in private; another thing entirely for those rantings to become police knowledge. Whether Grace knew it or not, this is why she had come to me — she couldn't be the traitor who betrayed her husband to the police in order to protect him, but I could be.

"He deserves to die," Rick said, sounding furious, paralyzed, sad.

"You bet," I agreed. "But you don't, and Grace doesn't deserve to be left alone if Heckler gets you first, or you get arrested."

"I can't get arrested, can I, just for wanting to kill him?"

"No, Rick, there's no law against that, yet."

"But this leaves him free to hurt Grace again!"

"It's my job to see that he doesn't."

Rick Kairn didn't sound convinced that I could do that, but then why should he, he didn't know me. I felt for him. When he asked me where Grace was, I said I couldn't tell him until I was absolutely sure that Jerry Heckler would never bother her again, no matter where she was. Kairn didn't like the mystery, probably half suspected me of kidnapping Grace, but he could see the point. If he didn't know where his wife was, he couldn't accidentally — or as the result of force — give that information away to Heckler. I wasn't worried about Heckler's friends, the ones who'd terrorized Grace and Rick with their messages that Heckler would "get her" when he got out; if they were going to do the job on her, they would have done it by now. No, Heckler sounded to me like a man who wants to take his pleasures for himself.

I assured Rick that I'd relay messages between Grace and him.

And then I got off the phone fast when I saw Jerry Heckler in the deli start to dig in his pants pockets for cash to pay for his supper.

When Heckler came back outside, I called out to him.

"Oh, sir!"

He turned, a beefy, red-haired, suspicious-faced man in his thirties, bumpy-skinned and heavy-lidded as a croc.

I advanced, holding a man's wallet out so he could see it.

"Did you leave this —"

"That ain't mine."

By then, I was close enough.

Strike first, but know your enemy.

"Grace," I said, low and clear. He looked startled, but then a corner of his mouth ticked, as if in amusement. "If anything happens to her or to her husband or to anybody she has ever met in her life, I will find you and I will kill you."

He laughed, at my appearance, at my threat.

"Yeah? What if something happens, and it's not my fault?"

He was having fun now, playing with his food.

"If I were you, I would work under the assumption that everything is your fault, Heckler."

He told me what to do with myself, his eyes on my chest, and then walked off, in no hurry to escape from me. But now I knew him: he was arrogant, unobservant, and careless, the kind of guy who never, never learns that he will get caught, which means he will not only do the time, he will do the crime.

What I said to him wasn't a warning.

Guys like that, they don't take warnings, because they have no restraint. The shrinks call it "low impulse control." No, what I was doing was making a positive identification and scouting behind the lines to protect my own rear.

I have high impulse control. I am very careful, at least I always have been. Now, with this cancer thing, something's coming loose.

I spent the subway ride home considering my choices and the consequences of them. When I was in the military, they took intelligent advantage of my best skill, which is exactly that — the ability to observe multiple opportunities and to foresee the consequences of all of them, quickly. It was a rare example of the armed services actually matching ability to assignment.

I spent only ten minutes at home setting up my plan.

First, I called Lt. Randolph.

"I talked to the husband, Janet. How about if I set up an appointment for him to go to your office?"

"Sure."

"When? You say."

"Tomorrow morning, ten-fifteen."

"I'll send him in."

Next, I called Grace's husband back, and told him.

44

"But I'll be at work —"

"Tell them something. You gotta be there, Rick. You have to convince her you won't harm a strand of Heckler's red hair."

He cursed me, but he agreed to do it.

I could have asked the lieutenant to call him to set up the appointment, but I had to hear his acquiescence, had to be sure he'd really make the appointment. Without mercy, I said to him, "Rick, I want to be able to tell your wife that Lt. Randolph actually saw you at ten-fifteen tomorrow morning."

That got him. "All right!" he said, shouting at me.

Last, I called Mom.

She said things were cool, and she said, "Grace is a nice woman."

"Absolutely. You taking her grocery shopping with you tomorrow morning, Mom?"

"Grocery — ?" She stopped herself. "Am I?"

"Big sale on at ten-fifteen. I'd get there before that, and then hang around a while afterward, introduce her to folks, let her see what a friendly little town you have up there."

"She'll want to move here, by the time I finish."

"That's fine."

"You take care, Daughter."

"Yes, ma'am."

My mother didn't know what I was up to, she rarely did anymore, but she was quick to *understand,* and you don't need facts for that. She used to tell me a story, drilled it into me, really, her favorite story from mythology. Where other girls heard about Snow White, I heard the one about Daphne and Apollo. Apollo's a god, Daphne's a wood nymph, and he wants her, but she runs away. Just when he's about to catch her, and she's desperate, she prays to her father, a river-god, for help. Her daddy, thinking he's doing a good thing, saves her by turning her into a tree. Thanks a lot, Dad. You couldn't turn Apollo into a tree, instead, and let your daughter run free? My mother always said the moral of this story is: Don't trust the fathers. Never ask the fathers for help. They will freeze you where you stand, always, to protect their precious status quo.

The inference was: When I need help, ask Mom.

I wasn't crazy about my own plan.

It was all more complicated than I liked, but I had a lot of alibis to arrange, my own included. I also had to work fast, because I couldn't stall Grace out of town forever. What I was planning to do was take Heckler out. Just like that. No farting around. Strike first. Set him up and take him out, in a way that protected Grace, Rick, and me from any suspicion. I was crossing a line here, a line I hadn't crossed since Vietnam.

The rest of the setup was easy, even enjoyable, requiring a couple of hours of scouting near the halfway house for a good shooting gallery, and a few hours of rehearsal with my clothing changes and with my equipment, to develop certain ambidextrous skills.

I went to sleep thinking about Vietnam. Bad move, resulting in weird dreams. By now, most everybody knows we had assassination squads working in country, but hardly anyone knows — and no one would believe it even if you showed them photographs, which I could — there were women involved. Let me put it this way: Not every peacenik who traveled to Hanoi was a pacifist, not every girl with a cross on her uniform was a nurse, not every female with a pencil was a journalist. This all happened, you understand, before I realized — it was a man vet who bitterly told me this — that all soldiers, especially draftees, are prisoners of their government. You don't believe me? Name one other job you can get shot for leaving.

I didn't dream about 'Nam, though.

I dreamed about my mother. She was coming toward me, smiling with determination, a bottle of almond-and-strawberry-scented shampoo in her hand. She was going to wash my hair. I really didn't want her to use that stuff on me, and I really didn't want her to get hold of my head.

I woke up screaming.

Then I lay there thinking — what a dramatic response to such a nothing little dream. My heart was thudding with fear and my upper body was slick with sweat. I put my hands on my chest right above where the X rays had shown the shadow, and I thought: Weird.

After that, I slept like a baby.

A cancerous baby.

When I awoke, I realized that being trained as an assassin is like knowing how to type: it's a skill you can always fall back on. Ever since I sensed what I was going to do about Jerry Heckler, I'd been thinking about him, but also about a certain child molester I read about who was released on a technicality, and about a terrorist who has somehow finagled his way into a minimum security prison.

I have debts from 'Nam.

And I'd been thinking, maybe I could pay them off — *pick* them off — one by one, starting with Heckler. Then I could write up my stories — like this one — and get them published anonymously to scare some of the bad guys. Let them start looking over their shoulders and wondering if they could be next. I was getting real excited about this plan. Like Mom always said: Angie, try to leave this world a better place than you found it.

Yes, ma'am.

I was almost laughing as I dressed, turning myself into a plain little wren of a woman. My equipment — sniper's rifle, telescopic scope, silencer, ammo, tripod, cellular telephone — disassembled quickly and fit perfectly into an ordinary straw bag that I had reinforced for strength. Over my first layer of camouflage, I slipped on thin plastic gloves, then put on coveralls, a well-padded jacket with a hood, a baseball cap with a long bill, and men's work shoes over my thin ladies' slippers. I'd already stashed a tool chest in my car after my practice sessions the night before.

As the old song advised: Walk like a man.

I would go up on the roof of a building across from the halfway house dressed as a workman with a tool chest. I would come down as a little wren with a straw bag, a woman so plain as to be nearly invisible.

It was a gorgeous day, chilly, sunny, no clouds.

And it was 9:45 A.M.

Up on the roof, at ten-fifteen, I called the halfway house on my cellular phone and told the man who answered that I was from the gas company and that we had a major gas leak on the block.

"Evacuate. Get everybody out now."

"Right!" he agreed. People can be so gullible.

Then I called the lieutenant and asked her if Rick Kairn was there yet.

"Sitting right here," she announced, sounding smug.

At that moment, Jerry Heckler walked out the front door of the halfway house. He was a big man, with a lovely large chest for aiming at, and I had ammo that would take down a grizzly, no mistake. I had to fire a cannonball, be-

48

cause silencers dissipate power.

"Tell me what you're telling him," I suggested to Janet.

As she did, I placed one finger of my left hand on the Mute button on my telephone and eased the trigger of the rifle with my right forefinger. Ambidextrous, for sure! And right then — at the worst possible moment in terms of the job — my memory kicked in.

It wasn't a Vietnam flashback.

What I remembered was that fear resides in an almond-shaped organ deep in the brain, the amygdala. Trigger that, and you trigger terror.

Terror. Heart pounding. Cold sweats.

Like my dream. Mom and the shampoo. The almond-and-strawberry-scented shampoo. I didn't know what the strawberry meant, but I knew the almond meant: fear.

Mom?

Shit! I didn't want to think about this now!

As she had warned me, I had never gone to "the fathers" for advice. Thousands of my male contemporaries had and they'd ended up in 'Nam. I had only gone to "the mothers." And here I was with a gun in my hand anyway.

I felt confused, paralyzed.

In that moment, with one finger on the Mute button . . . and Janet talking into my ear . . . and one eye on Jerry Heckler's chest . . . and another finger on a trigger, I felt empty as a jar.

Then I relighted, and fired the rifle.

When what noise there was subsided, I released the Mute button. And all the while, the lieutenant was telling me what she was telling Rick Kairn, who was seated right there in her office while his wife was being introduced to a dozen people fifty miles away. If the cops got suspicious enough of me to go to the trouble of tracking this cellular call, I was in deep shit. But, hey, I was already in deep shit according to several doctors, so what was a little more? Especially if I kept a crocodile from eating people?

Some days, everything works.

It all went perfectly.

Last week, I had lunch with Grace.

"We're safe, aren't we?" she asked me.

"Yes, at least from Heckler, I can't say about the rest of your life."

She smiled at me. "Thank you, however you did it."

"You're welcome. Now will you tell me what else you learned while you were dead?"

"I learned that we're already forgiven."

"Well, that *is* good news."

She laughed. "I learned that every evil act is actually a cry from the heart for healing, it is a plea to be reunited with God."

"Okay," I said, while she smiled at the skepticism on my face. "Then tell me this, who's God?"

She laughed again. "There's no 'who.' There's nothing — no thing — out there. It's all in here." Grace pointed to her chest, right about where my tumor is. "God is a name we give to love."

"Great bumper sticker," said I, tactless as ever.

But it seemed Grace wasn't defensive and I couldn't offend her. I decided not to mention that some scientists would say her near-death experience was merely a release of endorphins in the brain.

As usual, she was way ahead of me.

"You don't have to believe me, Angie."

"Okay, then if you don't mind, I won't."

We laughed, both of us, while I wondered why in the world I was resisting the idea that I could be forgiven for every bad

50

thing I had ever done. And then I knew why: because that would mean the Jerry Hecklers of the world were forgiven too.

I had called him, the evening after the morning when my shot had missed him by an inch. I had meant to kill him, had gone up on the roof to blast him. But in that instant when I stood empty — with the voices of both the mothers and the fathers silenced in my head — I changed my mind. I think that may have been the first truly independent act of my life, and I wish I could say I felt good about it.

"I told you not to mess with Grace," I said to him.

"I didn't do anything!" he protested. I knew he'd been frightened; I'd seen it in his face after my shot nearly hit him, after I'd purposely aimed off target.

"I know that," I told him. "That shot was for thinking about hurting her. Now consider what's going to happen if you *do* hurt her."

Maybe crocodiles don't take warnings, but they're not complete imbeciles. Even crocs will swim away to another swamp if they hear the sound of gunfire.

I was still worried about those other swamps, though.

"Jerry?" I said. "I'll be keeping tabs on you. If I hear that you are under suspicion for injuring any woman, not just Grace, I will come after you again."

"Who *are* you?"

"A good shot," I said, and hung up.

Who was I? A good question. I was no daddy's girl, and never had been. And now perhaps I was no longer my mother's girl, either. Who was I? A woman, empty, but for something shadowy growing in my breast. For once in my life, I can't foresee the consequences. But I know this natural law: Shadows cannot be cast in total darkness; where there is a shadow, there must be light.

Sign of the Times

Gentleman Joe had worked with some gorillas in his time, but this was ridiculous. This one was three hundred pounds of ugly and her name was Bubba.

"Good evening, dear," Joe said politely as he stepped into her house trailer that Friday night. "How's my girl?"

The nine-year-old lowland gorilla raised her massive head from the comfy nest of blankets where she slept in her cage. She opened one intelligent black eye, lifted the rubbery fingers of one hand and greeted Joe with an easily identifiable and definitely obscene gesture.

Joe's companion stared.

"Did that monkey just do what I think she did?" Melvin asked. His own blue, but not nearly so intelligent eyes widened. "I don't think she likes you, G.J."

"Nonsense." Joe entered his initials and the exact time in the logbook in which the university professors kept minute-by-minute track of the care and feeding of Bubba. She was rarely left alone or unguarded; a gap of only thirty seconds appeared between the time the last graduate student, a woman named Carole, had signed out and Joe signed in. He stepped over to the refrigerator, opened the door and looked over the tasty assortment of gorilla treats and vitamins. "Here, have a banana."

"Thanks." Melvin caught the fruit Joe tossed to him, but paused before he peeled it. "She's looking at me funny, Joe. Is this her banana?"

"Melvin." Joe spoke with the exaggerated patience one

uses with the lower orders. "Try to remember she's just an animal. Try to remember who's boss." He grabbed an apple for himself. Bubba's eyes fastened on its shiny red beauty; the thick fingers of her left hand moved in her right palm.

"Yeah, but ain't this the one what can talk?"

"She has a vocabulary, yes," Joe said loftily. "The professors have taught her sign language and she knows about six hundred-fifty words."

"Do any of them include get your hands off my banana or I'll kill you?"

Joe chuckled. He fastidiously picked gorilla hairs off the seat of Bubba's favorite easy chair and sat down. In her cage, Bubba's brows came down over her eyes. "You have the wrong idea about gorillas," Joe explained to Melvin. "They're strong, of course, but they're not mean. Bubba won't hurt you."

"If you say so." Melvin put the uneaten banana on the coffee table. He offered the gorilla a tense but conciliatory grin. She drew back her lips in a wide grin, too, showing off large teeth that were rather more white than Melvin's.

"See?" Gentleman Joe crunched down on the apple. "Now go back to sleep, Bubba, it's past your bedtime."

The gorilla obediently lowered her eyelids, though a glint of white continued to show between her lashes. She was accustomed to Joe's presence as her night guardian now that he'd been on the job a month. It was his probation officer who'd convinced the university to hire him based on the facts of his college degree and his reputation for having a peaceable — albeit greedy — nature.

"She's amazing, really," Joe lectured. "Or so the good professors say. Her 'talk' is not just a simple matter of saying yes, no, and feed me; any dog can communicate that much. Bubba's use of language extends even to abstractions."

53

He automatically answered the blank look on Melvin's face.

"I mean she can understand concepts like right and wrong, good and bad, happy and sad. You've just seen her insult me. She can also make jokes and even play games of pretend. She actually seems to *think*. She makes up words, she asks simple questions, and answers others correctly. What I find most astonishing is that she has a sense of time — past, present, and future. She can refer back to events and emotions that took place in the past, for instance."

Melvin looked dumbfounded.

"Do you mean to say," he demanded, "that tomorrow she'll remember we was here tonight?"

"Correct factually if not grammatically."

"And she'd be able to tell somebody that?"

"Very good, Melvin. You're nearly as perceptive as Bubba."

Melvin ignored the sarcasm. He grinned broadly and, this time, genuinely. "Well, my God, G.J., that there gives me an idea."

Joe grimaced at the solecism.

"Your last idea got me five years in Leavenworth, Melvin. Don't talk to me about your ideas."

"But you got out for good behavior."

"I *always* get out for good behavior." Joe crossed one leg of his crisply clean jeans over the other. He always had his jeans dry cleaned — hung, no starch — and his shirts professionally pressed, even if the luxury entailed other sacrifices. "A gentleman," as he frequently remarked, "has his priorities." His immaculate appearance was one reason for his nickname. Joe might be a thief, but he always looked the part of a gentleman. He said determinedly, "And now I'm going to stay out on good behavior."

54

Melvin's small eyes shifted.

"But G.J.," he said in syrupy tones, "there's a charity ball tonight."

"Do not tell me. I do not want to know." His specialty was robbing the kitty at charity fund-raising events; in his trademark tuxedo, Joe moved easily among the rich from whose burdened shoulders he liked to remove the worry of wealth.

"It's a fund raiser for the preservation of English opera. . . ."

"Dear God, who'd want to preserve that?"

". . . And they're having a money tree, Joe."

"You are a manipulative and despicable person, Melvin."

"This money tree is going to be seven feet high and the guests will stick their cash gifts onto it."

"Cash?"

"Yeah, no checks. It's a gimmick for publicity pictures. All that beautiful green cash, like a tree budding leaves in the spring."

Joe rolled his eyes at Melvin's flight of poetic fancy. He took the nearly nibbled core of his apple and deposited it in the garbage disposal. From the cage in the corner came a low growl.

"You imply it is harvest time," Joe inquired of Melvin, "and I the happy reaper?"

"No." His companion grinned and sprang his idea. *"I'm* the reaper this time. Listen, G.J., we've got the opportunity here for the world's most unusual alibi. I'll put on a tux and pull the job while you stay here with Bubba. I'll make sure the job has all the earmarks of one of your heists, so the cops will naturally assume it was you."

"Are you *crazy?*" Gentleman Joe's carefully cultivated aplomb shattered for a moment, revealing a hint of pure, unadulterated Bronx.

"Then when the cops come to question you, you'll have a witness to prove you was here all the time." Melvin leaned back in his chair in a most irritatingly superior way.

"Bubba?"

"You said she remembers the past, right? And she answers questions, right? And the professors will back up whatever their monkey says 'cause their scientific reputations are at stake, right? What have we got to lose? They'll never connect this job to me, and you'll have an alibi that's so weird it's got to be true."

Joe picked up Bubba's favorite red ball from the floor and bounced it thoughtfully from hand to hand. The gorilla's eyes followed the ball, back and forth, back and forth. "I really loathe English opera," Joe said finally. "Fifty-fifty split?"

"Agreed." Melvin grinned hugely. "Guess I'd better go climb into my monkey suit."

They laughed uproariously.

In her cozy nest, Bubba grinned, too.

"We know you did it, Joe." Approximately twenty-four hours later, the police detective was squeezed into the house trailer with Joe and two university professors, Dr. Andy Kline and Dr. LouAnn Frasier. They'd come quickly in the middle of the night at Joe's request. "This job has your name all over it in capital letters. Not much of a challenge, frankly. You're not as much fun as you used to be, G.J."

The professors stared.

"I was here the whole time," Joe said calmly. He smiled reassuringly at his employers, who smiled uneasily back at him. "I could not possibly have robbed a charity ball."

The detective also smiled. "Prove it."

"I have a witness."

"Who?"

Joe pointed at the gorilla in the cage.

At the cop's incredulous look, the professors hastened to provide a short course on language development and intelligence in the lowland gorilla. They were very convincing.

"Nobody could make this up," the detective said finally. He shook his head. "If that gorilla says you were here, it's just so damned weird, it's got to be true."

"Ask her," Joe said confidently.

"Doctor?" The detective turned to Dr. Kline. "Would you please grill your gorilla?"

"Certainly, officer." The professor sat down on the floor facing Bubba, who glanced alertly at each human in turn, lingering a moment on Joe.

"I'm asking her to identify that man," the professor explained as he began signing.

"Joe," was Bubba's reply, through the professor's translation. The cop looked impressed.

"She's crazy about me," Joe assured the detective.

"I'm asking her if she remembers last night," Dr. Kline continued.

"Yes," Bubba signed. "Bubba sleep."

"I'm asking who she saw last night."

"Carole," Bubba signed, and the professor explained that Carole was the graduate student who had the duty before Joe.

"Who else, Bubba?"

The moving, rubbery fingers paused. Then they signed.

"Nobody."

Gentleman Joe's heart began to pound to strange African rhythms.

"Nobody, Bubba?" Dr. Frasier broke in. "Joe was here last night, wasn't he?"

"No. Bubba alone. Bubba sad."

57

The professors and the detective stared accusingly at Joe.

"I was here!" he protested desperately. "She's lying!"

The cop turned a skeptical face to the professors. "Is that possible? Can *gorillas* lie?"

"Oh, yes," Dr. Kline said. Joe's heart settled back into a normal rhythm. "Interestingly enough, the ability to lie is proof of advanced capability in language and thought. I'm afraid Bubba can fib with the best — or worst — of us."

"However . . ." Something in Dr. Frasier's tone set Joe's palms to sweating again. ". . . gorillas are individuals, just as humans are, with distinct personality traits. Bubba, for instance, always tells the truth about people she likes."

"Oh, my God," Joe said weakly. An image of a certain obscene gesture floated through his mind, followed by an image of Melvin basking on a beach in Acapulco, followed by an image of a neatly wrapped parcel containing thousands of dollars in cash that was sitting on a shelf in Joe's apartment.

The cop's grin was as wide as Bubba's.

"You said it yourself, Joe." He smirked. "She's crazy about me, you said. So much for this monkey business of an alibi! Let's mosey on down to the station, shall we? And have a nice gentlemanly conversation about all those incriminating clues you left scattered around the scene of the crime."

He led a stumbling Gentleman Joe out the door to the waiting police car.

In the trailer, black rubbery fingers moved quietly in a palm.

"Bye, bye, Joe," they said.

Dust Devil

The father of the child pulled back the vertical blinds that hung at the window of his law office, and stared at the merciless sky that glared back at him from above downtown Kansas City. The sun was a branding iron, scorching the Midwest wherever its rays touched the earth. In this, the hottest August on record, the temperature had broken one hundred degrees for twenty-one days running. Newspapers warned parents not to leave their children or pets in cars, the city pools were so full a person couldn't dive under water without hitting somebody's legs, in airless rooms old people died for lack of fans.

The private investigator who was seated in the room inquired, "Look like it could rain?"

The man at the window, Chad Peters, didn't bother to answer the question that was on everybody's lips. He wasn't looking for rain. He was looking for his three-month-old son, Brook.

"My wife stole him from the hospital," Peters said, as if the private investigator hadn't spoken.

"Your wife's name?"

"Diane." His voice was hard and cracked, like the scorched earth, and it shook with a rage that rivaled the heat of the drought. "Diane Peters. If she's still using my name. If not, she might use her maiden name, Brewer. Diane Brewer. She was going to abort, but I got a court order preventing her from doing it. By the time her lawyers got that reversed, she was too far along in her pregnancy. And then what does she do, she steals the baby she didn't

59

want to begin with. I'm the one who wanted the baby, not her. My son Brook wouldn't be alive if it weren't for me. I don't even know if he is still alive. . . ." He let the blinds fall, plunging his office into artificial coolness and light, and he turned his face away.

The private investigator watched him. He judged Chad Peters to be around forty years old, already a full partner with his name on the door. Peters was tall, slim, a good-looking man, but not likable in his grief; he held himself upright and rigid as a dam, as if afraid that if somebody touched him it would poke a hole in his defenses, and all of his emotions would come rushing out in a drowning flood. The private investigator didn't like him, but he felt sorry for him, all the same. Losing a child to the other parent, that was tough on anybody. When the man had himself under control once again, he looked back at the private investigator. Peters's eyes were red-rimmed, but his flushed cheeks were dry, as if the heat of his anger had dried his tears before they could fall.

"Find them for me," he said. "I'll give you your advance, and expenses, and whatever it costs beyond that, but I'll tell you, the last investigator I hired took my money and ran with it. I never heard from him again after the first couple of phone calls. What I figure is that he found her, and that Diane talked him into letting her go. She's capable of that. Diane would screw an ax murderer if she thought it would hurt me somehow." His glance at the private investigator was aggressive, offensive. "How do I know you won't screw me, too?"

"You don't, but I won't."

Peters shrugged, as if he were past the point of expecting any good to come of anything. "What's your name again?"

"Ken, Mr. Peters. I'm Ken Meredith."

"I can't remember anything anymore. I don't know where to tell you to look, either. I'll give you the names of her family and friends, everything I gave the other guy, I'll give you any information you need, and I'll warn you as I warned him —"

Meredith cocked his head, always interested in warnings.

"Diane is nuts. She's an overgrown flower child, a twenty-seven-year-old hippie who's too young even to know what that means. She didn't want me, she didn't want our child. Too conventional. Too bourgeois. Of course, she also didn't want to use birth control pills while we were married," he said, bitterly. "Too much risk of cancer, she said. You run a greater risk of getting run over by a truck on the highway, I said. It's not your body, she said. Which is the same thing she said when I stopped her from having the abortion. It may not be my body, I said, but it's sure as hell my child. I don't know how far she'll go to spite me, but . . ." Peters shook his head. "I'm afraid. . . ."

"Of what, exactly?"

"That Diane will abandon my son. Or kill him."

"Kill her own child?"

There was a moment of silence, and then Peters said, "What do you think abortion is, Mr. Meredith?"

"What do I do when I find them?"

"Call me, but not if it means letting her out of your sight. If you so much as suspect that she'll run with him again, then take him."

"Steal the baby, just grab him? I can't —"

Peters interrupted him. "She has no rights."

Meredith was not convinced, but he thought of something else that settled the argument for him. "Okay, but it'll cost a lot more if I have to do it that way."

61

"Of course." The father of the child pulled back a slat of the vertical blinds and stared outside again. Meredith could barely hear his next words. "Everything costs more than you think it will."

The grandmother of the child, on the father's side, showed the private investigator her son's baby book.

"This is Chad as a baby, I'm showing you this because he looked just like my grandson. I got to see Brook in the hospital before she stole him away. Brook is a beautiful baby, just like his daddy was — look at all of that dark hair! I remember the doctor joking, he said, 'Mrs. Peters, if we'd given him a hair-cut you wouldn't have had to have a C-section!' Take this picture with you, Mr. Meredith. If you find a baby who looks like this, it's Brook." She was a young and pretty grandmother, and she gazed at him with sad hope in her eyes. "Maybe you could have some copies made? Put them up in truck stops, or something?"

"Where do you think she took him, Mrs. Peters?"

She sighed, and he watched the hope fade from her eyes as the breath escaped from her mouth. "If there were still such a thing as a Haight-Ashbury, she would have taken him there. She was so strange and emotional all the time, Mr. Meredith, I always suspected she must be on drugs. I don't know why Chad married her, although she's pretty, I'd have to say that she's very pretty. Chad always wanted a family, especially children. That could be one reason he married a woman so much younger than he is. And maybe he thought she was fun for a while, so much younger and freer in her behavior, you know."

She was working her wedding band, rubbing it up and down on her finger. Her eyes filled and her voice cracked on her next words.

"I think my worst fear is that she'll sell him, for money, for drugs."

"She isn't a very responsible person," her best friend confided to the private investigator as they sat together in her kitchen drinking sun tea from an iced pitcher she had set on the table between them. "I told the other guy that, too. I'll be straight with you, like I was with him. I love her like a sister, but she was always a little crazy. Like she'd fall for these guys, and she'd just move in with them after one date! Crazy. Nobody does that anymore. It's not . . . responsible. AIDS, and herpes and serial killers and all that. You can't trust people like you used to. But Diane always trusted everybody." Her mouth twisted into an expression of wry bitterness. "At least she did until she met Chad. He taught her that there are people in this world you can only trust to use you. He's like that, incredibly controlling. You'll do things Chad's way, or else. Diane was always so flaky, she must have looked like somebody he could mold, you know? Like turn her into this sweet, obedient little wife." The best friend looked up at Meredith, and laughed. "Boy, was he wrong."

"Why didn't she want to have the baby?"

"Why should she?"

"What?"

"I said, why should she want to have one?"

"I don't know. I thought every woman did."

"No." She didn't say it in an unfriendly way, but just as a statement of fact. He felt a little amazed at that.

"Then why did she keep it and run away with it?"

Her best friend smiled. "He was really cute."

"The baby? Is that the reason, because he was so cute?"

"I don't know, it could be. You probably think she's a

bad person because she didn't want to have a baby and because she wanted to abort it. But she isn't. She didn't love Chad and she didn't want to have a baby, especially with him, that's all. You could say that when she *met* her baby, she fell for him." Her best friend grinned. "I told you, she was always falling in love at first sight. So just because she didn't want him before doesn't mean she might not want him when he got here. Sure, she ran away with him, but it wouldn't be the first time she ran off with some guy."

Ken Meredith found himself feeling very confused, as if he'd wandered into a thicket of femaleness where he was lost without a map. He thought of the first PI, and pictured him running off with nutty Diane Peters and her baby. She'd keep him around only until they spent the money, that's what she'd do, and then she'd split again. Although, if she was half as good-looking as her pictures, maybe that wasn't such a bad way for a guy to make a fool of himself, even if it was just for just a little while. Meredith felt like laughing. The heat was getting to him, he decided. He sucked an ice cube into his mouth, to chill himself back into reality.

"But she took him away from his father," he said, talking around the melting cube.

"Well, of course," her best friend said, and then leaned forward to add patiently, as though to someone slow and stupid, "Chad's a lawyer, you know. Chad got custody, in the divorce settlement, and Diane gave up all visitation rights, because she didn't think she wanted the baby. He would have taken the baby away from her forever."

"The baby she didn't want, right?"

"Before. Not after." She screwed up her face so that she looked very intense, as if she were trying to convince him of something. "Mr. Meredith, can you imagine how it'd feel if other people *made* you grow a baby inside of you?" She touched her hands to her abdomen. "It'd be horrible." Her long fingernails scraped the fabric of her yellow shorts. "You'd feel like you wanted to tear it out of you with your bare hands."

"Then why didn't she just go ahead and abort it?"

"Chad told her he'd send her to prison."

Meredith doubted that could happen, but he wasn't sure, so he just said, "Where'd she go with the baby?"

The best friend leaned back, and grinned again. "I'm going to tell you?"

Meredith sighed. He wondered if the other PI had also felt like strangling this woman, if she had said that to him, too.

"No, really," she said, quickly, as if sensing that she'd gone too far. "Honestly, I don't know, although it's true that I wouldn't tell you if I did. But I don't, really."

"What's she using for money?"

The best friend shrugged. "From the divorce. And she's got a car, she could go a long way." The last phrase was accompanied by a swift, sly glance, as if she hoped to persuade him that it was useless to look.

"Mr. Peters is afraid she might abandon the baby."

She looked angry. "No way."

"His mother thinks she might sell the baby for drugs."

That produced a laugh. "Yeah, right."

"But you said yourself that she's irresponsible."

She rubbed her nose and thought about it. "I guess . . . I guess what I'm afraid of is that she won't have the sense to keep him out of this heat. What if she goes into a grocery store, or something, and she leaves him sleeping in her car? You know what she said to me one time? She said, I don't see why you couldn't just leave a baby in the house for ten

65

minutes while you ran to the grocery store. Can you believe that? My God, I told her, in ten minutes — less than that — a house could burn down!" The best friend nibbled on her lower lip. "What if Diane does something dumb like that? He could . . . die. . . ." She looked up at him, the laughter gone. "Okay. Well, I don't know where she went, but she loves nature. She always wanted to live on a farm, out in the country. You might look there."

He thought of all of the Midwest, most of it countryside, all of it baking under the 104-degree sun, and he shook his head, and smiled. "You couldn't be a little more specific?"

"Well, you might try the Flint Hills," she said. "Diane thinks it's beautiful out there." The best friend shuddered. "Gives me the creeps, all that open space."

"Thanks," he said, getting up. By advising him to "try the Flint Hills," she had narrowed it down to only about a couple of million acres of open country.

"How'd you get to be a private eye?" she asked him.

Abruptly, he sat down again The best friend was attractive and he was divorced and loathe to go out into the hundred-plus heat again. "I ought to warn you that I'm not really a very nice person," he said, surprising both of them. "What I do, sometimes it's shitty, like spying on un-suspecting people, like that. You might think, well, if a hus-band's playing around, he's got it coming, but you might be surprised to find out that he's the nice one, and the wife who hired me, she's the bitch. Or maybe it's the husband who hired me and he's a jerk, and his wife, the one I'm fol-lowing around, she's okay. But I'm working for whoever's paying me, that's the bottom line for me."

"You think Chad's a jerk?" she asked him, smiling a little.

"No, no, I didn't say that. You wouldn't have a beer, would you?"

★ ★ ★ ★ ★

Ken Meredith figured that the first investigator had also gotten a line on the possibility that the mother and child were hiding in the Flint Hills. According to Peters, the first guy had made his last report from a Rodeway Inn on I-35 at Emporia. Said he was following a lead. Meredith had laughed to himself when he heard that: sure, we're all following leads, even when we're sitting on our butts in air-conditioned motel rooms watching HBO. What the first guy had followed was the money, Meredith figured, and he'd followed it right on down the road.

In the first couple of days after getting the job from Chad Peters, Meredith followed his usual routine for disappearances: no moving violations had been issued to her in the three months she had been gone; she wasn't running up any credit card bills; if she was working, which he doubted, because of the infant, Social Security didn't show any sign of it yet. She had been the assistant manager of a health food store in Kansas City, and he doubted there were many of those in the meat-and-potatoes country of the Flint Hills. If she had been traveling alone, she might have been one of those adults who was nearly impossible to locate because she didn't want to be found. But as long as she kept the baby with her, he thought he had a chance of finding her. Babies needed diapers. And checkups and shots from doctors, maybe even medicine she'd have to buy from a pharmacy.

It was over one hundred degrees for the twenty-fourth day in a row when he drove southwest out of Kansas City. Even though he'd kept his car in his garage overnight, it didn't cool down enough to be comfortable until he reached Olathe. He wore a short-sleeved shirt and a tie, and his suit coat hung on a hanger in the backseat. On his way out of town, he stopped at a Kmart on Shawnee Mission Parkway and bought a car seat, a baby bottle, some formula, and a pacifier, just in case.

The farther south he drove, the farther away from city sprinklers and garden hoses, the drier and browner the state looked. When he stopped outside of Ottawa for an iced tea, he fancied he could smell the earth smoldering, heating up like a compost heap, slowly incinerating itself, smelling of dead baked grass and garbage. Meredith thought to himself: if we don't get rain soon, we'll be toast by September.

At the edge of the beginning of the Flint Hills, he started asking questions. He showed photographs of Diane and Brook to people working in the hospitals, pediatricians' offices, and drugstores in Emporia. When that netted him nothing, he drove deeper into the Flint Hills themselves, where the cattle listlessly swished flies with their tails at dry water holes.

He wished Diane had been deeply religious, so that he might have stood a chance of locating her through one of the many little churches that dotted the region. But unless you counted an interest in astrology, Diane wasn't religious, her husband had said, with a certain bitter wryness. If only she'd been Catholic, Chad Peters had said, and opposed to abortion, she'd have saved them all a lot of trouble. Just for the hell of it, and because you never knew where the oddest facts might lead you, Meredith bought a cheap horoscope book in a drugstore and looked up the Peterses' birth dates in an astrology book: Diane was an Aries and Chad was a Scorpio. The baby was a Cancer. The private investigator was amused to see that, according to the descriptions in the astrology book, it was no wonder that "flighty, passionate" Aries couldn't stay married to "cynical Scorpio." As for the baby, when he read that Cancers were supposed to love family, home, and hearth, he thought: fat chance for this child.

In Council Grove, near the site of a tree stump where there was a plaque commemorating the fact that General George Custer had rested there with his troops before charging on toward Little Big Horn, Meredith stopped at a grocery store for cigarettes.

More out of habit than hope, he showed the photographs to the clerk who checked him out.

"Oh yeah, I seen her, she come in here for diapers one time."

Meredith nearly laughed out loud. Wasn't it always the way that he found what he wanted when he wasn't really looking. All those nurses, all those pharmacists he'd quizzed, and none of them as helpful as this skinny girl with pimples standing beside the cash register and behind the jar of beef jerky. He could have reached across the *People* magazines and kissed her.

Still, he was afraid to hope for much; after all, Diane could have stopped here once before driving on to Texas, or New Mexico, or even old Mexico, for God's sake. But the clerk decided that yes, the woman with the baby had been back a second time. And then Meredith found a Texaco station where they'd changed a tire for her, and then a volunteer at a thrift shop recalled that a young woman looking like Diane's picture had purchased some baby clothes a few weeks ago. But it was at another grocery store, on the main street, that he made the discovery that settled the issue for him: about a month previously Diane had purchased several hundred dollars' worth of canned goods, diet Cokes, and other imperishables.

That told him she was staying around there, somewhere

within driving vicinity of Council Grove. To figure out where, he sought the help of the sheriff.

The sheriff showed Ken Meredith a map of the county and pointed out to him the locations of empty and abandoned buildings. "If she's not staying with friends someplace, or if somebody hasn't taken her in, then my bet is that she's holed up with the baby in one of these vacant places," the sheriff said. "Some of them are in falling-down condition, I mean she'd have to be crazy for sure to live in one of them, but one or two of them are nice places that belong to absentee landowners. Like this ranch —" He penciled an X on a thin line of road on the map. "I suppose she could be camped out, but I think somebody'd notice her, where they wouldn't necessarily if she kept inside of one of these old barns or houses."

By the time he was finished at the sheriff's office, Ken Meredith had a map and a list of rural addresses and directions on how to get to each place. He also had instructions to include the sheriff's office in any action he might be forced to take that might require legal, possibly armed, assistance.

It was easy, he thought, as he got back into his car, when you knew how to do it. He was so damned hot, though, and annoyed at this woman for running away and causing him so much aggravation in such miserable weather. He pictured himself spending the next days driving for miles over dirt and gravel roads, raising clouds of brown dust. What if his car overheated out in the middle of nowhere? What if he busted an oil pan or a tire?

Meredith could almost sympathize with the other private investigator for taking off with the money and saying to hell with the selfish bitch.

The mother of the child climbed the hill behind the

cabin every day, sometimes carrying Brook to the top in a papoose sack strapped to her back, other times climbing alone while the baby napped in the cabin. The hill was her Indian lookout, where she'd found an arrowhead that she wore around her neck on a string like an amulet.

The cabin she called her "safe" house. When she'd found it, it was empty except for a broken-leg table and a leftover wooden stool. Diane had cleaned its filthy kitchen, the bathroom, and all the rest of it. There she settled in with Brook, stocking the cupboards with the pans, food, and supplies she purchased after she fled from the hospital, making beds on the floor for both of them out of stolen hospital blankets and thrift store sheets.

Nobody bothered them. Sometimes she longed for the sound of traffic, for a telephone, and especially for a television. At those moments, she felt ashamed of her weakness. Then she reminded herself that she loved the cabin, its isolation, the eerie quiet, the pitch-dark nights that made her feel as if she were as courageous as the early prairie mothers.

She even loved the drought.

It seemed, on some days, to evaporate her, so that she felt as if she'd disappeared entirely. On other days, it baked her into a calm, stolid passivity that felt like endurance

"We're blessed," she whispered to the baby. "Thank the stars for these blessings, my little one."

The two of them, mother and child, had themselves and Diane's full breasts and canned goods in the cupboards and the cabin and the enveloping, comforting heat. During the days, she felt safe. But at night, waves of emotion — love, hate, fear — swept over Diane like terrifying, psychedelic waves of shimmering, pulsating heat.

One day after lunch, in the third month of their disappearance, when the baby was asleep in the cabin, Diane climbed to the top of the hill. The brown grass, hard and prickly as straight pins, crackled under her tennis shoes so that she felt as if she were climbing a tinfoil mountain.

As she climbed, the sun felt like a warm body pressed against her, sweating against her, and it filled her with a different, but very familiar, kind of longing. At the top, she stripped out of her halter top, her jeans, her panties, even her shoes. Stepping carefully on the flint pebbles and the grass that cut her feet, she stood on the hilltop, feeling like a tiny, invisible speck of life in an immense, dying landscape.

She could see no one.

No one could see her.

She lifted her arms above her head, so her hair fell down her back, and she closed her eyes and faced the sun. She hummed, the sort of tuneless song she thought an Indian woman might have hummed, a propitiation, and a prayer of gratitude to the sun.

The heat embraced her.

After a moment, she turned her face away from the sun and opened her eyes.

Down the dirt lane, dust was moving.

A deer? Diane lowered her arms to her sides, smiling at the thought of a deer — perhaps the antlered stag she had seen — and herself alone on the prairie, two natural creatures in a wilderness. . . .

The dust moved, and cleared, and she saw a man walking down the dirt road.

The shock of seeing a human being on the lane was so great that for a moment she didn't move. Then she dropped to the ground, wincing as the sharp grass and rocks bit her bare skin. Frantic with haste and fear, she worked herself back into the halter, jeans, and shoes, leaving the panties where they lay. When she looked up again, the man was closer, walking without any sound she could hear, keeping to the shade of the cottonwood trees, but coming steadily, as if he had a purpose in mind.

From behind the old tractor, with shaking hands and racing heart, she observed him.

He was tall, thin, with straight brown hair that shone when the sun hit it, as if it were greasy. The man wore city shoes and cheap-looking trousers and a short-sleeved blue shirt, opened three buttons at the neck so that his white T-shirt showed beneath it. He kept to the shadows, walking with his eyes on his shoes, except that every few seconds, he glanced up at the cabin. He didn't look at the top of the hill. Was that because he had already spied her there?

"Who are you?" she whispered, her mouth gone as dry as the ground around her.

With a single long stride, the man stepped out from the shade of the cottonwoods and began the long walk up the driveway. Diane strained to hear the sound of gravel under his shoes. Why would a stranger walk up her gravel drive in the middle of the broiling day? There were many possible reasons, but only one likely one. She stared at him so hard her eyes squinted to slits in the sun, as if she were trying to probe through that long skull into the reasons he held in his brain, as if she were trying to will him away, away! He had a long, tired face, and he looked angry, as if the heat had provoked him.

She watched him walk up the two steps to the back door.

Now he stood between her and the baby, and she felt it acutely. The three of them were in a line now — Diane crouching at the top of the rise, the stranger at the door, and the baby sleeping in the cabin.

Ken Meredith cupped his hands, making binoculars out

73

of them, and peered through the window that was set into the back door of the little cabin. He couldn't see into the dark interior, so he drew back and walked around the house, trying to look into the other windows. But they were all curtained against the sun. Or against somebody looking in them, and maybe seeing something hidden in there?

Instead of knocking, he placed his hand on the door knob.

"What are you doing!"

Startled, he turned quickly and looked toward the sound of the woman's voice. He saw her now, standing at the top of the rise behind the cabin. At first, he thought he was hallucinating in the heat, because what he thought he saw was a wild-haired, copper-skinned Indian woman above him. But then he saw that it was Diane Peters, all right, and that she was holding a good-sized rock in her right hand.

He held his hands high, open wide, to display innocence.

He had the unnerving feeling of having aroused something ancient and primitive from deep within the Flint Hills of the prairie. He was not normally an introspective man, or even a sensitive one, but Meredith knew fear when he saw it, and raw, dangerous fury.

He put down his hands, easily, appeasingly.

"Ran out of gas, ma'am. Use your phone?"

His heart beat twice before she said, "You'll have to go somewhere else."

The private investigator pretended to slump against the back door screen. "I don't think I can," he called tiredly up to her, and smiled as charmingly as he knew how. "Ma'am, I've already walked about five miles in these darned shoes, and if I don't get a drink of water, I'm going to die right here on your stoop. Please, if you could even make the call for me, I'll leave, and wait back down the road for the tow truck."

"I thought you said you ran out of gas."

He coughed into his hands before he squinted up at her again. "I don't know for sure that's the problem, ma'am. Could be a dead battery, or maybe it's just this heat that killed it, you know how cars are, they're like us people, can't take too much pressure." He smiled again, inviting her to smile down, to climb down the hill to him.

Instead, she shifted her weight, lifting the rock for a moment as she did so.

Instinctively, Meredith stepped back, though he tried to disguise the movement as meaningless and as casual as a man shaking dirt out of his shoe. But he knew that she had seen it and recognized that no man with just an empty gas tank on his mind would move so quickly, so defensively.

"Go away," she said in a tough voice.

He pursed his lips, as if he were thinking that over, but then he shook his head at her, almost sadly, as if he were disappointed in her.

The man suddenly cocked his head toward the cabin.

Oh my God, Diane thought, he's heard the baby.

One of his hands disappeared from her view, and she realized he was opening the cabin door.

Through the open windows, filtered through the curtains and the dusty screens, came the crying sounds of a baby waking up. The man shot her a look that had cunning in it. Quickly, he turned his back on her and faced the door.

"No!" Diane screamed. "Stay out of there!"

She ran down the hill at him, and reached the stoop just as he was about to shut the door in her face. Diane shoved her weight at the door, forcing it open.

"Damn, lady!"

The door pushed Meredith backward, and he was laughing a little, as though in astonishment at her strength.

75

"Now hold on, Diane, let's just talk about this. . . ." His arms flew up to protect his head as she flung herself at him with the rock. "Your husband's got a right to see his baby. . . ."

The baby began to wail in the bedroom.

"No!" She brought the rock down on the side of Meredith's face. Blood ran into his eyes, blinding him, and then into his open, astonished mouth, choking him. "No, no, no!" with every scream, she struck him, until he slumped to the floor.

Her hands lost their strength, and the rock fell out of them.

The man was still breathing.

After a moment, Diane stepped over him.

She washed her hands at the sink, and then ran to the screaming baby. With the stranger out of her sight, around the bend of the L-shaped room, she nursed Brook back to tranquillity.

"I will never let anyone take you away from me."

She whispered it over and over, in a singsong, like a lullaby.

The idea had come to her as she had lain in her own blood on the delivery table, the very moment they placed at her breast the baby that Chad had forced her to bear, and which he would force her to give up forever. She had stared at the tiny face and thought: this is what Chad wants more than anything else in the world. And suddenly she had known what to do. She would take the baby. By· running away with the child, she could make Chad suffer every day for the rest of his life. Lying on the delivery table with the baby in her arms, filled with hatred for her ex-husband, Diane had felt a stirring of love for the child, as unexpected as a lily floating in a pool of acid. She also experienced an orgasmic-like rush of the vicious, soul-deep satisfaction of perfect revenge. She vowed: no one will ever take this child away from me.

Nobody. Ever.

While the baby kicked his legs happily on the cabin floor, Diane pulled the unconscious man deep into the cold, damp darkness of the storm cellar where the other man's body lay, and then she walked out and bolted the door. This time, she didn't take his wallet to see what his name was, or how old he was, or to see if he had any pictures in his wallet of a wife or little children. This time she didn't want to know anything about him, not even if he carried a private investigator's license, like the first one. She did remove his keys, however, and then set out walking until she found his car a half mile down the road. She drove it into the same barn where her own car was stored, and then abandoned the vehicles to the owls and rats. Back at the cabin, Diane scrubbed the linoleum floor, while her jeans and halter top soaked in cold water in the sink.

In the morning, the baby giggled at the sight of the deer in the pasture.

The drought carried on into September.

In Kansas City, Chad Peters hired a third private eye, this one a former cop by the name of Ed Banks.

In the country, every day after lunch, Diane climbed the rise behind the house. The heat was such that she began taking her clothes off inside the cabin and going naked into the afternoon. The sun baked her skin to brown and warmed the milk in her heavy breasts.

At the top of the rise, she raised her arms to the sun, her hair fell down her back like an Indian blanket, and she closed her eyes. When she opened them, she gazed down, looking for dust devils blowing up the long dirt road.

77

STORM WARNINGS

When a bad storm approached on the prairie, it came roiling in from the west like a furious posse on huge black horses. All her life, Elizabeth Randolph had loved those storms. They made her heart pound and her stomach clench and her skin prickle. In the electric moments before it arrived, a storm made her feel like her lover was coming and she hardly had time to wash up. It made her feel like she was twenty instead of fifty and that there was plenty of time for her time to come. At the first lick of wind, Elizabeth would run to the porch to stare toward the west, imagining those towering black clouds were coming to carry her away from the farm, like Dorothy in *The Wizard of Oz*. When the storm passed, she always felt limp, sad, and a little privately disappointed that it hadn't swept her off her feet and slammed her against the barn and damn near killed her.

In the days before she met Ed Cuddy face-to-face for the first time, Elizabeth felt as if just such a storm was blowing into her life. She hoped she wouldn't be disappointed. She hoped this quiet man would be the whirlwind that swept her out of Kansas forever.

"What do you look like, Elizabeth?" he said to her over the phone the day before they were going to meet for the first time.

"Like you think a tall woman looks."

He laughed. "Tall, you mean?"

"No, like the picture in your mind." She almost wished

they never had to meet, that they could just carry on by phone forever. "Angular. Elbows. Neck. Wrists. You know."

He chuckled again, but she heard a pause that told her how he'd imagined her.

"Well, I guess I'll know you when I see you, Elizabeth," he said in a gently teasing tone. "I'll just look for the woman with the elbows and neck and wrists."

"You'll recognize me, Ed." And then she boldly added, "We'd know each other anywhere."

He had been a wrong number and they'd started talking.

"Oh, I'm afraid I've dialed wrong," he said apologetically. So many people aren't apologetic, Elizabeth knew from experience. When such people get a wrong number and you tell them so, they just hang up on you. Or they demand to know what *your* number is, as if it's any business of theirs. So she noticed when the unfamiliar male voice said, "I hope I haven't bothered you. I'm awfully sorry."

"What number do you want?"

"555-4575."

"This is 4577."

"Ah, well, I dialed a seven instead of a five."

"I've done that. It's an easy thing to do."

"I am sorry, though." He sounded quite nice and sincere. "I hope I didn't disturb your evening."

"Not at all, that's all right."

"Thanks very much. Good-bye."

Neither of them had seemed to want to hang up.

He called again the next night and then every night after that. She had a nice voice, he said. He also said right away that he was married and lived in town. He hoped he wasn't bothering her.

"I don't imagine it will do any harm," she said.

By the fifth call, she knew his name was Edwin P. Cuddy. Her name was Elizabeth Randolph and she lived alone on the farm now, she told him.

"Mother died three years ago," Elizabeth explained. "With her and Dad both gone, it's been hard."

"I *am* sorry," he said. She appreciated the respectful pause of a couple of seconds before he spoke again. "You run the place by yourself, do you, Elizabeth?"

"Well, I don't suppose you'd say I *run* this place," she told him in a rueful tone. "I keep a garden, of course, but the rest of it I lease out to a fellow for his cattle."

What she didn't say was that she had told the "fellow" — Richard Jackson — about her caller and that she and Jackson discussed him every evening when Jackson stopped by for coffee after hard days of selling his cattle to early spring buyers.

Jackson took to asking, "How's your gentleman caller?" It always made her smile. Jackson, who'd known Elizabeth's father, advised her strongly to consider what her father would have thought of the situation.

"This Cuddy sounds all right to me," Jackson finally observed one day, much to Elizabeth's pleasure. "If your dad were here, I think he'd approve."

"Mother wouldn't, though," she said.

"Well, no, of course not."

As the calls continued every night, Elizabeth began to eat her supper early, so she'd have the kitchen all cleaned up by the time Ed phoned from the store at six o'clock. She began to take her baths in the afternoons, instead of just before she went to bed at night. She'd pour in bubble bath and lie back, dreaming, until the bubbles disappeared and the water cooled. At about four forty-five, she'd climb out of the old porcelain claw-foot tub and towel herself dry. Then she'd pat on dusting powder, drawing the puff under her arms and beneath her breasts and between them, and then patting it between her legs and on the bottoms of her feet. When she was dressed again in a clean blouse and slacks, she'd sit at the vanity table in her bedroom and fool with her long black hair, even though it always ended up pulled into a chignon at the back of her head. She wondered if she should dye the gray out of it. In honor of spring and hope, Elizabeth took to poking sprigs of wildflowers into her hair.

Elizabeth even told the banty hens about Ed.

"His name is Ed," she informed them as she sprinkled feed on the ground for them. "He's sixty-three years old. And he doesn't have a happy marriage. And he works in a farm-implement store in Duncan." Once she said to the hens, "I don't know if he can take a joke." She pronounced it *yoke*. "I'll have to ask him!" That amused her so much that she had to sit down on a rock wall and laugh while the chickens scrabbled around her feet and gabbled as if they enjoyed the pun.

On a Thursday, after two weeks of "wrong numbers," there were tornado warnings for both of their counties. Edwin called early that evening, just to be sure she knew. He called again after the storm, when the air seemed to her to be as clear and clean as freshly washed glass. It was then that he suggested they meet.

"I only have a half hour for lunch most days," he said. She smiled to herself at the gentlemanly tone of apology with which he expressed regret that it was she who would have to drive in to meet him. She didn't mind, she said truthfully, she was happy to do it.

On Friday, she walked nervously out of the sunshine and into the cool of the café where they'd agreed to meet. It was, she was relieved to see, clean, respectable, and out of the way, a place where a man who happened to be married could meet a friend who happened to be female without giving rise to gossip. Surely, no one would even remember having seen them there together. Anyway, none of the "help" or the customers would recognize her, since she neither lived nor shopped in Duncan. Elizabeth looked around for a man sitting alone. She located him in a green vinyl-covered booth against a wall.

"Edwin?" she nearly whispered it.

"Elizabeth?" He stood up so fast, he spilled a little of his coffee. She grabbed napkins to help him wipe it up, and soon they were laughing and settling back into opposite sides of the booth.

She tried not to stare at him.

"I guess you thought I'd look different," he said with a self-deprecating smile. It was true that his hair was thinner than she'd imagined, and not combed very neatly. But then the wind was blowing hard outside, as it always did in May in Kansas. He was wearing a yellow-and-blue-striped polyester short-sleeved shirt and a yellow tie; his blue trousers were the type that didn't require a belt but seemed to be held in place merely by the force of his paunch against his waistband.

His eyes, however, were blue and sincere.

After only a moment or so, Elizabeth relaxed, feeling sure that he was the man of character that she and Richard Jackson had agreed he must be. Just the sort of man of whom her father would have approved.

Over lunch — he ordered the roast beef special, after which she did, too — Ed told her he needed her advice.

"I feel I can trust your opinion," he said.

An investment opportunity had come his way, he said, involving natural-gas wells.

"Well," Elizabeth said, "my father always said a man had to be careful when he drilled for oil or gas, because he might only come up with hot air." She was glad to see him smile at that. "My father, I should tell you, was a fool about money."

"That's exactly what I don't want to be, Elizabeth."

And yet, he confided, it did seem such an attractive investment, with a really astonishing rate of return. He'd even heard that several of the wealthiest people in the county had put their money into it. But, he said, he didn't know how he could manage it, since a fellow needed to be able to put down $25,000 in cash right away.

"Oh, my," she breathed.

He admitted — and she saw that it pained him, for he was a proud man — that he did not have $25,000 to invest. "I might be able to scrape $15,000 together. I do have that much put away toward retirement."

"Ed," she said, feeling wonderful and light, "I have $10,000 my parents left me. I want you to take all of it and add it to your funds and make the investment for *us*."

"No," he protested, "I couldn't!"

"Yes, really, I insist."

"But, my dear —" He looked so startled at his own use of the intimate words that she smiled at him. "I mean, oh, my dear Elizabeth, I'm overwhelmed by your trust and by the generosity of your heart."

Ed called the farm-implement store where he worked to tell them he'd be late coming back from lunch. Then he let

Elizabeth drive him to her bank in the town of Bennett and he waited in her car while she drew out the money. She made a charming little ceremony out of handing over to him the $10,000 in cash.

Ed sat for a moment with the money in his lap. When he looked up at Elizabeth, she could have sworn there were tears in his blue eyes. He lifted his brown vinyl briefcase from the floor and carefully tucked the money inside it.

"Elizabeth," he said in a husky voice. "Dear Elizabeth, my dear wrong number, would it be all right if I kissed you?"

At her shy nod, he kissed her on her left cheek.

"Good-bye, dear Elizabeth," he said when he got out of her car back at the café. His eyes were so bright, she had to look away from him. "I'll call you right after I meet with the gas man to give him the money." He got out of her car, the briefcase clasped firmly in his right hand.

That afternoon there were tornado warnings again. The electric excitement of the impending storm sparked Elizabeth's own inner eagerness until she could barely stand to wait for Ed's call. She didn't even try to enjoy a bath, but took a quick shower instead. The time for dreaming was done; now was the time for her dreams to come true. When the phone finally rang at six-thirty P.M., she nearly dropped it in her rush to answer.

"Elizabeth?"

He didn't begin by saying playfully, as he had every other evening, "Do I have the wrong number?" His voice sounded heavy and strange.

"Ed? What's wrong?"

"Oh, my God, Elizabeth." She had never before heard him swear. Then suddenly, horribly, he was weeping. She

84

imagined his face all screwed up, his shoulders sagging, his free hand flung to his forehead in a melodramatic gesture of despair.

"I don't know how to tell you," he said.

But he found a way, through his tears. He hated to tell her, he hated himself. It was all his fault, he'd never forgive himself. They had lost all their money, all $15,000 of his retirement savings and all of the $10,000 her parents had left her. Yes, he'd met with the gas man, and yes, they'd exchanged cash for papers. But the papers were worthless! There wasn't any gas well! The scoundrel had lied, had suckered him and skipped town with their money.

"How do you know?"

"Because he's gone, Elizabeth. Oh, my God in heaven. I tried to call him at his motel to ask him a question and they had never heard of him. Whoever he was, he's gone now. I don't know how to find him again, Elizabeth. I'd better go to the sheriff."

"Sure." Her voice sounded as bright and hard as the real world is after a sweet dream. "And you tell him how you called me up every night for weeks and how you got to know all about me. And how you got me to trust you and give you my money. And you tell him about this famous gas man that nobody but you has ever seen on the face of this earth. And how this fellow just disappears into thin air. You just go ahead and tell him that, Ed, or whatever your name is!"

"Elizabeth!"

"Don't you bother about the sheriff." She began to weep along with him, in sobs so loud and harsh, they hardly sounded human or even real. "*I'll* see the sheriff. You'd better believe I'll see the sheriff!"

"No!" Now he sounded frightened. He had no proof of

85

his innocent intent, he said. He begged her to believe he never meant to hurt her. He begged her not to drag his family into scandal.

And in the end, in a dead and defeated-sounding voice, Elizabeth told him she would not go to the police — that she knew she had no proof of his guilt — but that he must never tell a living soul what a fool she'd been. He must never call her or speak of her again. After having practically seduced her and taken every cent she had in the world, she said, that was surely the least she could ask of him. She loathed him when he continued to weep and to call out her name until she hung up on him.

When she turned from the phone, she heard the radio announcer warning all residents of the county to take cover immediately.

Elizabeth ran to the window to look out, and then she ran out of the house, onto the side porch, and stared up at the oily, greenish-black fist of a sky, from which a single thick finger dipped low in the distance. She watched the fat black finger curl and straighten, curl and straighten, seeming to beckon to her.

"Come on and get me!"

The wind slapped the porch swing back and forth wildly against the house. Elizabeth ran down the porch steps. The wind flipped her skirts about her and whipped the flowers out of her hair and flung them in her face. She ran toward the weaning pasture behind the cattle pens. The rain began to pour. Breathless, soaked, she raced for the cabin in the pasture.

"Richard!"

The tornado was coming, roaring like a locomotive now, and her scream seemed to disappear under the tracks.

She barged into the one-room shack and stood dripping

86

on the threshold. Here was where Jackson lived during the months he worked the cattle on the land he had leased from her father and then from her.

"Jackson?"

His clothes and shaving kit were gone from the pine shelves in the corner. The potbellied stove was there, and the cot. But it was stripped bare. His clothes were gone.

In the face of the stripped and abandoned cabin, Elizabeth got the picture. If there was a sucker born every minute, she was this minute's fool.

Jackson was gone.

Jackson, who'd been selling off his cattle earlier than usual, was gone. With his big promises and plans. With Ed Cuddy's money and with her money, which was only supposed to have been used as bait. With his talk of how even her father would have approved of the scam.

Now Jackson's words reverberated in her head: "Your dad always said to find somebody who's old and lonely. Make him trust you and want you, then take the sucker for all he's worth."

How many nights had she lain awake fantasizing of them, of Richard Jackson and her, running away together with the money, running somewhere, away from all these miles of nothing, nothing . . .

Elizabeth stumbled out of the barren cabin into a suddenly dead, still world. In the eerie, malevolent moment before the twister struck, Elizabeth's wild and triumphant glee shattered into panic.

"Jackson!" she screamed. *"You bastard!"*

She started running again, with the twister roaring behind her, both of them aiming for the dead cottonwood tree that stood on the highest point of the pasture.

Elizabeth reached it first and turned around, pinning her

back against the dead tree to watch the tornado come and get her. As it roared closer, she began to laugh. Weakly at first, then wildly, hysterically. *Jackson found himself somebody who was feeling old and lonely, Dad, just like you said, and he got her to trust him and want him, and then he took the sucker for all she was worth.* The world was flying into a million pieces and soon she would be one of them. . . .

But the tornado, like Jackson, failed her.

It passed behind the cabin, sucked an abandoned outhouse into its obscene, churning bowels, and veered off away from the cottonwood tree on a crazy skitter to the northeast. Elizabeth stood with her back to the tree for a long time, until the rain stopped and the storm disappeared behind her.

SEX AND VIOLENCE

The call came at 10:30 on a Saturday morning in January.

When her phone rang, Amy Giddens was still in her white chenille bathrobe, seated in her rocking chair in front of her gas fireplace, her slippered feet up on a hassock. She was drinking coffee and reading *The Kansas City Star*; the crumbs of a croissant lay on a plate on the floor beside her. A fragrance of bayberry rose from a fat green candle on the hearth; a scent of cinnamon drifted into the living room from a pot of apple cider that simmered on the stove.

She picked up the phone and said hello.

"Oh, Amy, something awful has happened."

It was her friend, Kathy Weltner.

Amy sat straight up, sweeping the newspaper off her lap.

"Of all people," Kathy said. "I mean, I thought he'd live forever. Oh, Amy, Ross Powell is dead." Her voice broke. "I knew you'd want to know. It's just so . . . unbelievable."

Inside her, Amy's voice cried, *No*.

As she listened to Kathy, she stared out her own picture window, noticing in some part of her consciousness that this was just the kind of gray, bitterly cold day that would have inspired Ross Powell to take off for some place like Portugal, where the sun was always shining. She felt a big, lonely emptiness begin to inflate her body, and into the emptiness there poured the huge, silent *No*.

She managed to inquire: how, where, what happened?

"He drove over a cliff." Kathy laughed a little wildly, but

the sound got snagged on her tears. "In France. Above Monte Carlo. I mean, of course. Like Princess Grace. Oh God. It's not funny. But if he had to go, I'll bet this is how he'd want to do it, except maybe if he could have had a heart attack while he was fucking, that would have been even better. Maybe that's how he drove off the cliff." Again, she half laughed, half cried, "It would have been just like him, wouldn't it?"

At the word "France," Amy was jolted by a wave of nostalgia so strong that it shocked her. It was three years since she'd seen him, but at that moment she remembered Ross as clearly, as vibrantly, as if he were that moment leaning over her, just as he had towered over the Europeans in the train stations. He was so much taller than most of them that she'd always been able to spot him easily in crowds. She saw his shoulders, such all-American male shoulders, that strained the leather of the jacket he bought in Spain; and his arms, which were longer than normal, giving him a simian, disproportionate appearance that you couldn't detect face-on, but which you caught sometimes when you glanced at him out of the corner of your eye; and the curly brown hair that hadn't looked so rebellious in Europe where so many other men also wore ponytails; and his mustache that drooped to the corner of his mouth when he frowned; and his lips and nose that were too large for the rest of his face, giving him a lazy, sensuous look; and his hazel eyes that held a woman's for a promising, tantalizing moment before sliding away, as if he knew a sexy secret or had told her a lie. In that startling, vivid instant, Amy could even smell him, and the greatest shock was remembering that his after-shave had smelled like bayberry, just like her favorite kind of candles.

"Amy? Are you there . . . are you all right?"

The memory disappeared. Amy wanted to cry out: *No! Wait!*

"When did it happen?" she managed to say.

"Last week. I heard it from somebody who heard it from his mother. They say it was at night, and they think he was alone —"

"Think?"

"Well, the car just sailed off a cliff into the Mediterranean. They say he probably died on impact, instead of drowning, although they won't know for sure until they find, oh God, his body. So it was probably instantaneous. I hope. I can't bear to think how he felt on the way down, can you?"

"So there's no funeral?" Amy felt as if she had to pull her voice up from deep inside a great, hollow well.

"His mother will hold a memorial service of some kind, I guess, but we're having everybody over here tonight for a sort of party in his honor. I know you didn't care about him anymore. And I know he was such a jerk to you. But he was *Ross,* you know? And everybody from the old days will be here. And they'll all want to see you. So you'll come, won't you, Amy?"

She promised to.

After she put the receiver down, Amy stared into her real fire burning between her phony logs. And it was at that moment that her memories began, as if by some sort of romantic, nostalgic alchemy, to transform themselves from bitter into sweet. *He was in a good mood that last morning in Albufiera. And earlier, he had looked so sexy, so tempting, lying asleep in their room. What if she had slid back into bed with him? What if she had smiled back at him at the café, forgiven him, kept traveling with him? Would he still be alive?*

Five years ago . . .

91

Outside the drawn curtains of their hotel room in Albufiera, the morning sun struck the rough surfaces of the whitewashed buildings like a match, shooting fierce sparks into the cool air. A thin beam of light filtered through the muslin and lay like a warm dime on Amy's cheek. Her mind came reluctantly awake before her eyes opened; it took a few foggy moments for her to comprehend the nature of the unexpected heat on her face.

Sun? she thought, unbelieving.

She was afraid to open her eyes and look for fear this blessing might fade back to darkness in her dreams. She squeezed her eyelids tighter and prayed to whatever gods had been harassing her, Let that be the sun shining. Then she opened her eyes cautiously, only to snap them shut when the glare hurt them. Blessed pain.

"Thank you," she murmured into her pillow.

Amy lay still in the expanding pool of warmth, and listened for sounds from the other side of the bed. Ross was breathing deeply, but he wasn't snoring. He never snored. It was one of those qualities of his for which she had continued to try to feel grateful. He was funny, when he wasn't depressed, that was another one. He was tall. Charming to strangers. Kind to dogs. "Arf," she said softly, and stifled a giggle. God knew she'd wagged her tail for him. "Arf, arf."

And he was incredibly patient when she made major blunders — like the time she left her passport on a table in a cafeteria in Paris — even if almost everything else she did annoyed him. One memorable night, he'd been angry because she left food on her plate. Food on her plate, for God's sake, as if she were five years old!

"I'll order the child's plate next time," she'd snapped back.

"Well, that would be appropriate in more ways than

one," he'd said coolly, so that she'd had to bite back the tears that would have seemed to him to prove his point.

In point of fact, she was twenty-six and he was thirty-one. His life was devoted to finding jobs that paid enough for nine months to allow him to escape to the south of Europe every winter; her life, for the past two years, had been devoted to saving enough money to join him this time. It had been, mostly, a disastrous idea, she had finally admitted to herself: she couldn't get close enough to him; he couldn't get far enough away from her.

But this is this morning, Amy thought, lying in bed, and the sun is shining. It was not a trivial thought, she knew; in long, cold, gray winters, the sun was never trivial, and its promises were not to be taken lightly.

Amy still had not opened her eyes again, but at least she knew where she was. No small accomplishment that, considering the rate they'd been traveling. "I am on the Algarve," she recited reassuringly to herself, "in the south of Portugal, on the Iberian Peninsula, on the continent of Europe, northern and western hemispheres, third planet from the sun." She smiled. "No wonder it took so long to get here."

Then she discovered another miracle.

She put a doubting hand to her abdomen just to be sure; she pushed in, then out. No cramps, no nausea. Her stomach had unclenched itself in the night.

She'd been the sickest two nights before, in Lisbon.

"Maybe I'll die," she'd told Ross, and had imagined a flicker of hope in his eyes. "For heaven's sake, go to dinner without me."

"I'll bring you back something," he'd offered, looking resentful. Then without waiting for a reply, he had rendered the offer meaningless. "I'll probably stop for a drink, so don't wait up for me."

"I'm not likely to do that," she'd said, dryly.

It seemed to her that everything she said lately was dry, as if to compensate for the eternal rain. Or, possibly, because she herself had condensed. When she met strangers on the road, she wondered if they could tell she had turned into a block of dry ice, expelling lifeless steam instead of air.

Ross had returned to their room after midnight when she was aching with fever and wretched from hours of diarrhea and vomiting.

He had not inquired about her health.

"I found a wonderful bar," he'd exclaimed, full of the energy of his evening. Rapidly, he'd stripped down to naked, talking all the while. "In the old part of town, down this wonderful windy street, all cobblestones. And there was a Fado singer you would have been crazy about, all melancholy and kind of haunting. I met this old guy there —"

He'd jabbered on while she'd huddled in a fetal position, resenting the hell out of him, yet glad that he was talking to her again, and smiling. She was worn down by the mercurial changes in his temperament, depressed one week, manic the next. And he accused her of being emotional! Was he crazy? she wondered as she lay aching, or just selfish? If he was crazy, as in truly mentally ill, did she have to feel sorry for him and keep loving him? If he was just selfish, *could* she stop loving him?

And then he'd crawled into the bed and pressed himself against her burning back. He'd wanted sex. She was too sick and weak to fight about it, and so she'd let him do it. And hated him.

Finally, she'd hated him.

Months later, she confided to a friend about that night in Lisbon, and was surprised and embarrassed when the friend called it "shocking," and said he had "raped" her. "Oh no,"

Amy protested, "I could have said no, and he wouldn't have done it, it isn't the same thing at all, I'm sorry I ever said anything about it, and please don't tell anybody else, okay?" After that, she didn't confide to anybody certain things about her relationship with Ross. Like the time they were screaming at each other in their room, after too much beer, in a hotel in Germany, and the manager intervened because she said that Ross was so much bigger than Amy that the manager was afraid "the little American girl" might get hurt. He never would have done that, Amy, thoroughly mortified, told the woman; he would never lay a hand on her in violence. And he certainly never had, except for that time in Florence when he slapped her when she cried hysterically because he hadn't spoken to her in five days. But that didn't count, and besides, it worked. She stopped weeping and he started talking. They'd been cooped up together too much, that was all. And that German manager, she was just overreacting out of some sort of guilt left over from World War II, Amy figured out, that was all, like maybe she hadn't protested when the Nazis took her Jewish neighbors away, or something like that. Anyway, that was her problem, not Amy's or Ross's.

Maybe it's the weather that makes us crazy, she thought as she lay in bed, in Albufiera, as the sun radiated into her vital organs.

They'd been weeks in search of the sun, or was it years? They'd chased its winter shadow from London down to the Atlantic. But even on the road from Lisbon, it had rained and they'd despaired of ever feeling warm again. Amy had wrapped herself in a blanket that Ross had stolen from their hotel and she had huddled in the passenger seat of the rented car and shivered with the flu. All the way along the two-lane blacktop, through green fields of black olive trees, she'd shivered. Past square, one-room houses painted brilliant pastel colors that shone fluorescent in the rain, she had shivered and sweated into the scratchy wool. Halfway, they got stuck behind a funeral cortege. The coffin, a simple wooden affair loaded onto the flatbed of a clean truck, was trailed by somber men on motorcycles and squat, walking women in black. Amy had gotten the feeling she was the corpse and the world was mourning. Knowing better, but playing for sympathy, she'd confided her hallucination to Ross. He'd suggested it was time for her to take another Tylenol. . . .

She slipped out from under her covers and stood beside him, staring down at him in bed. One or two people had told her he reminded them of the actor James Coburn. In the sunlight, Amy examined the long, lean body that gave him that look, and the high cheekbones and the wide mouth, and the creases around his eyes that hinted at intelligence and cruel wit.

"I've known you to be gentle," she whispered. "I've even known you to be kind."

But not lately.

He slept snorelessly on.

She padded barefoot across the rug to her suitcase to scoop up underwear, slacks, and a shirt. Then she went quietly into the bathroom to shower and dress, anxious to avoid the heat of his glance on her nakedness. She didn't want him to want her this morning. Most of all, she didn't want to want him.

A few minutes later, before she left their room, she looked back at it. It appeared so elegant to Amy, and it was cheap, to boot. God, she loved Europe. She had yearned to come here almost as much as she had desired to be with Ross this winter. And now here she was, existing on two different planes — still thrilled by the journey, but miserable with loneliness and resentment. She knew she would never have taken this trip without him; basically, she was a sedentary person, not an adventurer like Ross. Loving him had freed her to do this extraordinary thing — to quit her job and to travel for three months in Europe. Without him, she wouldn't have had the nerve. If she left him, she wouldn't have the courage to continue traveling by herself, she'd probably fly straight home, and even the thought of managing *that* by herself made her feel sick with nervousness. They were both free, and yet he felt imprisoned by her presence and she felt imprisoned by her own fear. Weird. In the bed, Ross moved an arm. Amy quickly, quietly, closed the door.

Ross found her two hours later on the veranda of the big luxury hotel on the beach. The sun was just coming over the building, and there was a slight breeze, so the morning wasn't really all that warm yet; Amy was glad that she'd slipped a sweater on over her shirt and jeans. The Atlantic Ocean, looking gray and restless, was only a strip of beach away from her table. She had known that Ross would have to wander in this direction to find breakfast.

"Hi," he said, and smiled down at her.

"Hi."

He leaned down to kiss her, lingering a moment on her lips, so she knew this day he would honor her with the privilege of one of his good moods.

He dragged a chair up to her table in a rectangle of sun, put an exuberant arm around her shoulders, and hugged her with every evidence of fondness.

"Café au lait," he said to the waiter. "I mean, *con leche.*" He laughed, as if the waiter and Amy would enjoy his predicament, and threw up his hands. "Christ, what country is

97

this? Which language this morning?"

The waiter didn't appear to get the joke.

"Can you believe this glorious day?" Ross squinted into the sunshine, looking as pleased as if the day had been especially arranged for him.

She put a finger in her mystery novel, and closed it.

"Yes, it's wonderful."

"How're you feeling?"

"Okay. Good."

"Thought you were going to die on me."

"I felt like it, I guess."

He gazed at her appraisingly, but in a friendly way, over his steaming coffee cup. "You look better," he said finally, and then he grinned. "Good enough to eat."

"Try a croissant, instead," she said, and felt the steam come off the dry ice again.

He leaned back in his chair, and laughed.

"Listen," he said suddenly, eagerly, like a small boy with a big plan. He grabbed her free hand and squeezed it. "How about if we take the car and drive on down the coast for the day? Maybe have lunch on the beach somewhere, get some wine and cheese, what do you say?"

"Ross," she said, then bit her lip.

"All right!" He released her hand, then leaned back again, appearing satisfied with the state of things. "All right."

No! Amy's voice cried inside her head: *It isn't all right!*

"Ross?"

"What?" Was there a hint of awareness, a suspicion at the back of his eyes? Then he smiled again, and whatever she thought she read in his glance was gone. "What, honey?"

"I can't stand —" *to ride your roller coaster again! Stop it! Or let me off!* But for a moment, she lost her nerve.

"What can't you stand? You don't want to go to the beach? It'll be gorgeous. What?"

"Nothing."

"Oh, that!" he teased. "Well, that's nothing."

"Ross?"

"What?" He laughed. "What, *what?*"

"Nothing." Suddenly she was furious, at him, at herself. *I'm getting off, damn you!* "I'm leaving, I'm getting off!"

He looked utterly surprised, and the beginning of angry. How could she ruin their day? he'd demand to know. How could she throw a stupid, goddamned tantrum on a gorgeous day like this? What in the hell was the matter with her?

"Nothing!" she said, and other customers turned to look. *"Nothing!"* As Ross stared at her, Amy pushed back from the table, threw down her napkin, and ran from the veranda.

She slowed to a walk near their hotel.

There would be buses returning to Lisbon that very day. And from Lisbon there would be planes to carry her home. She hadn't meant to do it this way, but it was better than . . . nothing. Yes, she was frightened, but a smile was growing on her face. *It is,* she thought, *so good to leave on a sunny day when the world is bright and clear and sharp.* The winter sun was strong and hot on her back, like a warm, moist hand, pushing her. . . .

It was the last time she saw Ross.

She thought she had left him forever. She thought she had left herself with only a healthy residue of bitter memories of a selfish man. She had married somebody else, and divorced that man. Dated other men, broken a couple of hearts, and suffered her own being broken again.

But five years later, upon hearing that Ross Powell was dead, Amy was awash in a passionate, sentimental longing for him. He'd been so much fun, she'd loved him so much, and she felt sure that he'd cared about her too, in his own strange way, that maybe he'd even loved her more than he'd ever loved any other woman, and that he'd missed her terribly when she was gone, and that he was sorry for all the times . . .

Oh, God, if only she could love him one more time.

He couldn't be dead. No!

Although she hated the idea of what the party represented — that he was really dead — she couldn't stay away.

Kathy Weltner and Sam DeLucca had married in the old days when the whole gang, including Ross and Amy, worked as copywriters or artists in the advertising department of Macy's, back when there was a Macy's in Kansas City. There'd been many pairings back then, but Sam and Kathy were the only two who were still a couple.

"It's your three kids that keep you together," proclaimed Steve Allison, as he set down his contribution to the evening: a case of Budweiser, which was Ross Powell's favorite back in the good old days. "You can't either of you bear the thought of being left alone with the kids."

"Not a problem Ross ever had," Sam DeLucca observed, his dry wit still intact after all those years. "God love him."

"At least not that we ever knew," his wife, Kathy Weltner, added in her own tartly distinctive style, which had also distinguished her writing. "It's difficult for me to believe, however, that there aren't a few little Rosses — or Rossettes — scattered about the globe, you know?"

"God, what a terrifying thought," said Lara Eisenstein, who was still an advertising illustrator in town. "I loved him, too, but . . . clones of Ross? Mothers, hide your daughters."

"My theory," Steve said, as he popped the tops on Budweisers for each of them, "is that he didn't accidentally go over that cliff at all. He was too good a driver. So I figure a woman killed him. It's only logical —"

"Inevitable, you mean," Sam said, and they all laughed.

"Not to mention justifiable," Kathy interjected.

"Okay," Steve said, "so maybe it was that one who went after him with a knife that time, remember her? What was her name? Or the other one — the accountant — who rammed her car into the back of his. And then into the front. On purpose. And there was that lady, God, poor thing, who tried to kill herself when Ross left her." He took a swig of Bud, wiped his mouth, and smiled. "I think one of them pushed him over the cliff, and who could blame them?"

"Maybe they all got together and did it," somebody called in from the living room. "All the women he ever dumped. You know, like that Agatha Christie mystery, what was it called? *Murder on the Orient Express*? Where they all took a stab, pardon the pun, at the victim?"

"They never called *me*," Amy said.

Sam DeLucca laughed loud enough for his amusement to carry in to the gang in the living room. "Ross, as victim? You expect us to buy that? No way! Ross was a penetrator . . . excuse me . . . perpetrator if there ever was one!"

"Very funny," his wife said. "You're all wrong, anyway. It was a jealous husband or boyfriend."

"Couldn't be," Lara Eisenstein objected. "Ross never dated married women. Remember? It was a principle of his —"

"Principle!" Sam and Kathy hooted at the same time,

and Kathy added, "The man hadn't seen a principal since he left high school."

Lara laughed, and made a face at them. "No, really, I mean it was a prin-ci-ple of his never to date married women because . . ." She looked around at each of them, smiling, and shaking her head. "Why should he mess with that kind of trouble, when there were so many other women who were so utterly available to him?"

Kathy suddenly turned toward Amy. "Oops. Listen, guys, maybe this is not tactful. I mean, obviously, it's tasteless, which is only fitting considering the subject, but maybe it's also tactless? You want we should shut up about Ross and his other women, Amy?"

"Don't be silly," Amy said, "it's history."

"I don't get it," Steve said. "How could a man who wouldn't hurt a flea inspire so much violence in so many women? I always thought he was kind of a gentle guy, you know? I mean, he was a good friend, loyal, do anything for you, give you the shirt off his back —"

"Big deal," Sam laughed. "Kmart special, all polyester."

Steve laughed, too, but he said, insistently, "All right, but you know what I mean. He was a hell of a lot of fun to be around. I thought he was a nice guy." He took another drink of Bud. "So there, asshole."

"He was nice if you were his friend," Kathy said, in a reflective tone of voice. "That's true. Although he could drive you crazy, the way he used to just drop by any time of day or night, like just when we would be trying to get the kids to sleep. But for his girlfriends" — she glanced at Amy with a smile full of sympathy — "I think there was a lot of wear and tear."

Lara Eisenstein laughed. "You make him sound like a Laundromat."

"I'll tell you what I could never understand." Sam affected a woebegone expression that made him look like his own golden retriever. "What was it about him that attracted women like flies? Begging your pardon, ladies. But I mean it was like they were the flies and he was the screen door. Or they were the flies and he was the garbage . . . no, no, I didn't mean that, that can't be right. Do you understand it, Stevie? Hell, he wasn't even good-looking. What did he have that we don't have?"

The women in both rooms smirked, with the exception of Amy, and one of the men in the living room called out, "You had to ask, dummy!"

"He had glamour," Kathy said. "And style. All of those trips to Europe. Those sports cars he drove, because he didn't have to pay for a mortgage or for preschool like the rest of us. What was attractive about Ross was the life he led, which consisted of periods of compulsive responsibility interspersed with total abandon and adventure. Like a Yuppie Indiana Jones." Her smile was self-deprecating. "I guess it's obvious that I've been thinking about it a lot since he died." Suddenly there were tears in her eyes and in the eyes of several other people there, as well. "Ross was bigger than life. Shouldn't that mean that he wasn't supposed to die?"

Sam slapped his beer can angrily down on his kitchen counter. "What the hell was he doing there, anyway? Wasn't he getting a little old for that stuff?"

"He'd been working for one of those Texas savings and loan companies," Steve said. "One of the ones that went belly up. I think he took his last paycheck and said, adios, guys, have a good time in court, I'm off to Europe."

There was a moment of silence in both the kitchen and the living room. Finally, somebody said, "Let's pretend he's not dead, he's just late to the party."

"Okay then, here," said Steve, holding high a Budweiser, "this is to the late Ross Powell, who's going to walk in that door any minute now and tell us it was all a joke on us. Ha." He drained his beer and then set the can quietly on the counter. "Ha." In a choked voice, he said, "Well, he hated winter, and now he'll never have to see it again. It'll always be summer on the Riviera for Ross."

"We agreed that he wasn't really dead," Sam snapped at him. "He's merely late to the party, probably out picking up a woman somewhere. So cut the sentimental crap. Shut up and drink."

Later, when they had a moment alone in the bathroom, Kathy said to Amy, "You're so quiet. Are you feeling just too sad? Are you okay?"

"I'm not sad," Amy said, and it was true, she wasn't. What she was, was excited. She didn't have to pretend, as the rest of them did. In her heart, she was beginning to feel it was true: Ross couldn't be dead, because he *wasn't* dead. It really *was* unbelievable that he could be dead . . . because it literally . . . wasn't . . . true. They might play around with the idea of what had "really" happened to him, but she had known him better, more intimately, than any of them ever had, and she knew that only she was able to put the facts together to fit the only possible conclusion. *Fact one: they'd found a car but no body. Fact two: he'd walked off with money from the failed savings and loan company in Texas, probably more than they knew, possibly even a lot of it, and he may have even stolen it. Fact three: if that were so, it would have been just like him to stage his ultimate escape.*

It was all she could do to restrain herself from grabbing Kathy and hugging her and exclaiming, "I think he's alive! And I can find him!"

★ ★ ★ ★ ★

Once she had the notion, she couldn't shake it.

Driving to work, eating lunch with her friends, talking on the phone to her mother, going to the bathroom, taking a shower, putting on makeup — at all times, a part of her mind was doubting. That he was dead. Hoping. That he was alive. Figuring out. How it could be possible. Dreaming. What she might do about it.

Amy didn't say a word about what she was thinking to anybody, not even to Kathy. She knew that anybody she might confide in would think she was nuts; worse, they'd say she was still in love with him, and they'd feel sorry for her.

Well, maybe she was still in love with him.

But they didn't need to pity her.

They should envy me, Amy thought when she had it all figured out, *because I'm the only one of them — of his friends, of his family, of all of the people who ever knew him — who may get one more chance to see him again.*

Deep down, she wondered — she fantasized — about how he might, by now, be desperately hungry to connect with somebody who really knew him, about how glad he'd be to see her again, about how he might invite her to slip inside his new life, to start all over again with him now that they were older and wiser, about how he might beg her to share his last, best escape.

But most of the time she told herself she only wanted to see him. One more time. One last time. It would be a sort of triumph, a sort of victory, a trick on the trickster, but one that would surely make him laugh the hardest of all. It amused Amy so much to think: I escaped from you, lover, but you can't escape from me.

At work, they only knew that Amy Giddens took her regular two-week vacation and flew off for a glamorous fort-night to Europe. Cyprus. Torremolinos. The Canary Islands. The Algarve. They looked at her travel folders and envied her exotic, sun-stroked itinerary, marveling at the stamina it would take to visit so many wonderful places in so short a time, and at the adventurous spirit that propelled her to make this trip by herself. A few bluenoses at the of-fice sniffed at her spendthrift manner of throwing money away on an outrageously expensive vacation. Amy stared at those same travel folders and saw Ross Powell's favorite destinations in his search for never-ending summer.

On the airplane, she kept thinking: there are so many places he could be, places she remembered that he had liked, places where the sun always shone, like almost any-place along the Riviera, Morocco, Tunisia, Majorca. But the most likely place was Albufiera, because nobody Ross ever knew was ever likely to go there, and because Portugal was still cheap compared with the rest of Europe. Amy re-membered Albufiera as a town where the only noticeable foreigners were German and British; Americans preferred the resorts north of Lisbon instead of the Algarve to the south.

And, she had to admit to herself, she *wanted* it to be Albufiera. Because it was beautiful, and because its beauty and her melancholy had made her heart ache, and because she had left him sitting there, and it would be so natural to walk back into the café, at the hotel on the ocean, and to find him sitting there again, to go up to his table, to smile as he had smiled at her and to say, "Hi. Can you believe this gorgeous day? Let's take the car and drive on down the beach. We can stop for a bottle of wine, some bread and cheese, what do you say?"

When she thought of how Albufiera looked, she remembered a particular arch that separated the street from the luxury hotel. In her memory, the street was cobblestones; the hotel had no remembered shape at all. But the arch was vivid in its particularity in her memory: lovely in its simplicity, thick as a man's arm from wrist to shoulder, rounded like the innermost curve of a woman's neck; the sun cast half of it in shadow, the other half in light so bright the whiteness of the arch made her eyes hurt when she remembered it; and what she remembered most of all — whether or not it had actually been true — was that when you stepped through the arch you moved out of cool, sad shadow into the light.

Amy's plane landed in Lisbon on a Monday morning. She drove, in a rented car, all the way to Albufiera that afternoon, arriving at dusk.

Leaving her bags in the car, she walked first to the beach where she and Ross had hung out to watch the sun set over the Atlantic Ocean. Just as she had remembered, the Portuguese fishermen were pulling in their nets from their brilliantly painted little boats. Women sold glittering silver fish out of buckets set up on wooden tables in the sand. There were tourists there with lighter skin and hair, and men who were taller and thinner than the Portuguese, but none of them was Ross Powell.

As the sunset grew ever more violently pink and orange, Amy abandoned the beach and walked toward a little dinner restaurant that still lived in her memory. It had been frequented by foreigners, and the tables had been so close together that you couldn't help but get to know your neighbors. But when she thought she found the right location, she saw only a gift store selling knickknacks.

It was dark by the time she found the hotel where they'd stayed, and she wasn't surprised when the clerk told her that no Mr. Powell was registered there. Of course, Ross wouldn't use his real name, she realized. She was expecting that problem. But the clerk also volunteered that there were no Americans at the hotel at all. "Australians?" she asked. No, none of those. "English, Scottish . . ." She began to feel foolish, inquiring of various nationalities under which Ross might be hiding. The clerk grew impatient, and resorted to claiming that she didn't speak English, which of course she had been, if haltingly, until that very moment.

"Oh God," Amy said to herself as she left the hotel. "If I'm wrong . . ."

It would be an expensive mistake, not only in terms of her limited funds but also in the amount of time she had in which to look for him. There were so many places he could be, all of them hot and sunny, except . . .

She remembered a bar — long and cool and dim, even in the daytime — manned by a British expatriate who called out your name the second time you came in, and who paid you the compliment of talking to you in a humorous, cynical way about tourists, as if you weren't one. It was a bar where at any time you could find Germans, Scandinavians, British, and Americans, and always somebody who spoke English. Foreigners stuck together in Portugal, she believed, because they felt like time travelers in an earlier century. The natives either didn't or wouldn't speak English, and the English didn't speak Portuguese, which was so different, so separate from Spanish; everybody stuck to their own kind, staring at the others, and wondering, but rarely pushing through the door from one culture into the other. It was such a good place to hide, she knew it was, and she knew that Ross would think so, too. Here, everybody seemed to be hiding something, some secret — the Portuguese, most of all, hiding their glances, their language, and their souls from the foreign tourists, and most of all, hiding their curiosity. They asked no questions, they gave nothing away in their dark faces: perfect people to hide among, because they appeared to take no interest at all in their visitors.

She was willing to bet the English bar owner would still be mixing drinks behind the counter and welcoming strangers as if they were regulars. So what if Ross wasn't at the beach, and so what if that restaurant was gone now? There were cafés where Ross might be eating dinner this very evening.

But first she would try to find that old bar.

Amy stepped into the cool, dim interior of the bar and scanned the length of the room. She didn't see the Englishman. That depressed her so that she was ready to give up and go find a room for the night. Then her heart lurched and she nearly cried out when she noticed the man seated on the last stool at the end. He was tall, too thin, with a full beard and a mustache; he'd brushed his hair back off his forehead and it fell, curly and unbound to his shoulders — which looked too wide in proportion to the rest of his body. His profile, as he raised a glass of beer to his mouth, displayed a wide nose and full lips. He was wearing a battered brown leather jacket over a black turtleneck sweater and well-worn blue jeans.

Amy ducked, so that she could observe the man at the end of the bar without being seen. Was it Ross? It couldn't really be! Suddenly, for the first time, Amy was struck by the absurdity, the absolute unlikelihood of her quest. Ross Powell was dead. He was supposed to be dead, he wasn't supposed to be sitting here, in the same bar where they'd sat together five years before. And even if he was still alive, it wasn't possible that she had really found him. Out of an entire world of places to hide, she couldn't have picked the one. It wasn't possible, this wasn't the man, she was out of her mind, and she ought to face that truth, have a quick drink, go back and pack her bags and go home, clear-eyed and sane once more.

He turned his face in her direction.

It was undeniably Ross Powell.

And he saw her, looking at him.

After the first instant of surprise, he smiled.

His lips moved as if he were saying something to her, and he pushed his weight forward on the palm of his left hand, as if he were going to push himself off of the bar stool and come toward her.

"Wine!" A woman shoved her way to the bar directly in front of Ross, and she was followed by two other women. "We'd like a carafe of red wine, please."

Amy couldn't see Ross behind the women.

And then the women were joined by three men, and all of them bunched up jovially at the bar, arguing loudly and good-naturedly over whether to order wine or beer.

Rooted to the floor by the shock of actually seeing him, Amy waited for him to get off his bar stool and walk around the crowd and come over to her. When he didn't appear, she took a couple of tentative steps in his direction.

But then the party of six separated enough for her to see that the bar stool behind them was empty. One of the women noticed, and sat down on it.

"Ross?"

A man at the bar turned to stare at her.

Amy hurried forward.

He was gone. Nowhere in the bar. There were some Portuguese coins thrown down on the counter beside his half-finished drink.

Amy started to hurry out the door, to chase him into the night, to find him and grab him.

But was it really Ross she had seen?

Leaving the bar, she wasn't sure any longer.

Such a quick glimpse, after so many years . . .

But that *smile* . . .

Amy stumbled out of the cool, dim bar into the even colder, even darker Portuguese night. And suddenly, she was also aware of how alone she was: a woman alone outside of a bar in a strange country. She suddenly wanted to get back safely to her car, and to find a hotel room quickly.

That smile. *It* was *him. She knew it.*

She'd look for Ross again tomorrow.

Amy slowed down. Or maybe she wouldn't. If he'd stolen money from the savings and loan, if he'd faked his own death, he wouldn't want to be found, not even by her. How could she have been so foolish as to think he would?

She walked into the dark, narrow street that led in the direction of her car. She felt desolate, stupid. And suddenly, frighteningly, she felt as if she were being followed. Amy picked up her pace until she was nearly running.

She heard footsteps running behind her, drawing nearer.

If she screamed, in this foreign country, where everybody ignored her, would anybody help her?

Amy felt a hand land roughly on her back. It pushed her off balance, shoved her into an alley beside the bar. She cried out as it grasped her shoulder and whirled her around.

"Ross!"

She was staring into his face as he grabbed her hair and pulled her head back. Her eyes were still open as he leaned down and kissed her, forcing her mouth open, pushing his tongue between her teeth, shoving her body against the brick wall.

Her eyes closed as she felt his hands meet in a circle around her neck.

The Dead Past

At first, she was only a new name in the appointment book of the psychologist, Paul Laner, PhD.:

"March 3, Tues., 12:10, Ouvray, Elizabeth"

Then she was a lovely girl in the doorway of his office, young and slim, pale as a ghost, wearing gray trousers and sweater, and her platinum hair caught up at the sides of her scalp with translucent plastic barrettes. Her beauty, Laner thought at the time, was the stunning natural kind that is formidable to look upon, and which instantly forms a wall that other people have to scale in order to reach the person behind it. According to the form she had filled out for his receptionist, Elizabeth Ouvray was nineteen years old. Laner, at forty-five, was old enough to be her father, and he felt at least that much more mature than she as he stared at the nervous, ghost-like girl in his doorway.

Indeed, like a ghost who was afraid to materialize, she hesitated, her head down, eyes averted. She looked to him as if she wished she were invisible. Her hair, parted in the middle, hung down from the barrettes like curtains pulled over her face.

"Come in," he said.

She glanced up at him, and smiled stiffly, slightly, as if any facial expression were an effort. Instinctively, Laner wanted to put his hand under her elbow and lead her gently into his office, but he didn't. The doctor was careful not to touch her, not only because Elizabeth Ouvray looked as if she would flee at the slightest overture, but also because the hand of a male counselor on a female client could be so easily misinterpreted. A comforting pat on the shoulder, a gently intended squeeze of the hand could get even a well-respected psychologist like him into serious trouble.

She scooted past him without speaking, leaving in her wake a lemony scent that made his jaws ache. Saliva pooled on his tongue, and he swallowed. She was, easily, the best looking patient to walk through his doorway in his twenty-three years of professional counseling. He thought it poignant that a woman so blessed in her physical appearance should appear to feel so cursed. Following that thought, Laner experienced such an immediate and intense desire to find out *why* she felt cursed that he experienced a mild sexual arousal.

"Down boy," he commanded his libido. "Sublimate."

Behind her back, he smiled to himself. It pleased him that after all this time in his career he could still get excited about the human mysteries that awaited his unraveling.

"Sit anywhere you like," he suggested to her.

He observed her as she made the difficult and meaningful choice that faced every new client: whether to sit on the couch in the corner farthest away from him, or the Windsor chair midway between the couch and his desk, or in the rocking chair beside his desk. She finally chose the latter — not, he thought, because she was self-confident enough to sit that close to him or because she craved intimacy, or even because she had a bad back. Rather, he suspected, it was because she felt safer there than she would have felt all the way across the room by herself. The doctor couldn't help but make an instantaneous diagnosis in layman's terms: *fear* — stark, staring, trembling, not-quite-raving fear. This clearly neurotic young woman was afraid of her own shadow.

Laner smiled inwardly at his own Jungian pun.

He felt a warm surge of hope for this new patient and an even warmer surge of self confidence. Eagerly, almost buoyantly, he crossed the room and sat down at his desk, facing her. Sensing that small talk would not relax this patient who had yet to utter a word to him, he launched right in.

"How can I help you, Elizabeth?"

She didn't hesitate, but said in a soft voice, "I'm afraid."

Laner was surprised at her directness. But taking that as a cue, he proceeded to be extremely direct and clear with her, himself.

"What are you afraid of, Elizabeth?"

"Everything." She didn't smile when she said it.

"All right. Tell me one thing that frightens you."

"Coming here."

"Yes, everybody's nervous the first time."

Laner purposely cultivated a fatherly appearance in order to put his clients at ease. He knew that when she looked at him she saw a nice, middle-aged man with frazzled gray hair, a friendly, bushy moustache and beard, a man with bright, intelligent and intense blue eyes and a tactful, sympathetic smile.

He presented that smile to her. "What else?"

"I'm not *just* nervous," she protested, as if he had belittled her complaint. Her near-whisper had a defensive, annoyed edge to it. *What was this?* he wondered. Was she proud of her neurosis, (many patients secretly were) or did she already have resources of courage and independence with which to defend herself? That would be a hopeful sign for her prognosis, he thought.

"I believe you," he said quickly. "What else scares you, Elizabeth?"

115

"People," she said, and he was inwardly amused to see that she was looking suspiciously, even furtively at him. "Strangers."

"I see. What else scares you?"

"Oh God, you name it!" she burst out. "I think I'm really crazy. I must be crazy to be so frightened all the time."

"Nobody is afraid for no reason, Elizabeth," he told her. "My experience tells me that we will discover that your fears are the natural, if perhaps rather exaggerated, effects of certain causes. Our job will be to uncover those causes, so that we may eliminate the effects of them. You understand what I'm saying?"

"Yes, but it sounds too . . . easy."

"Would it make you feel better if I assure you that it probably won't be easy?" He smiled at her. "We often find that the greater the fear, the more deeply buried the cause. I will help you, Elizabeth, but I can almost guarantee that it will not be in one easy lesson."

"You'll help me?"

"I will," he said firmly, and was delighted to see the relieved expression in her eyes, and the slight relaxation of her tense body. "Tell me, Elizabeth, do you feel scared all of the time?"

"Yes! Every minute. All the time."

"Right now?"

"Yes!"

"How does that affect your life?"

There was anguish in her eyes. "It ruins it."

"How does it ruin it?"

"I don't want to be around anybody. I don't want to go out, I don't want to go anyplace. I don't date. I've never had many friends. I was in college, but I quit, and now I just get up in the morning, I go to work, I go home, and I stay at home until it's time to go to work in the morning."

"Not much of a life," Laner commented, gently.

She began to cry. "No, it's not much of a life."

He encouraged her to weep the sadness out. In truth, at that point, he foresaw a long and difficult therapy, but he was not for a minute afraid of failing her.

First, the psychologist attempted conventional therapy, fully expecting it to work.

He began by administering psychological tests, which served to confirm his original hypothesis that Elizabeth was deeply neurotic due to abnormally deep-seated fears of undetermined origin. Or, as he commented privately to his wife, "The poor girl's scared shitless."

Twice weekly, he asked probing questions and Elizabeth reacted, sometimes calmly, sometimes decidedly not. But none of them was the *right* question; none of her answers was *the* answer. Sometimes Laner felt she was telling him the truth; other times, not.

"Tell me about your mother, Elizabeth," he said.

"She raised me by herself."

"Where was your father?"

"Pretending I didn't exist."

"Tell me how you felt about school, Elizabeth," he suggested. ". . . about God, Elizabeth . . . about men . . . tell me about your dreams, Elizabeth . . . your daydreams, your fantasies. Tell me, Elizabeth . . ."

Over time, it became clear that she was not getting better. Instead, to his dismay, she grew progressively worse. Her appearance disintegrated. Laner grieved at the loss of her remarkable beauty, at her frightening weight loss, at the acne that ruined her beautiful skin, at her humped, defensive posture, and the sad, gray cast to her eyes.

"I've quit my job," she announced one day.

She lost her insurance, and couldn't pay his bills.

Laner adjusted his sliding scale to compensate, until finally he was treating her for free, something he had always sworn he would never do for clients because it would increase their dependency on him and destroy one of their main motivations to change.

"You're taking this case awfully hard," his wife finally said. What she really meant, he knew, was that he was taking it too personally. "Watch it, Paul," his colleagues warned, "you're becoming obsessed by this case." Their comments infuriated him, although he couldn't deny them. But he couldn't quite believe them, either.

It was not conceivable that Dr. Paul Laner could so miserably and completely fail to help one of his patients. No one, he thought, would be able to comprehend it, least of all him. "I'm a *good* psychologist," he kept telling himself; in fact, the peer recognition he had achieved over a long career suggested that many considered him to be a great one. But the doctor began to sleep less well, and to be aware of vague, unpleasant stirrings in his chest and abdomen. He did not need a psychiatrist to diagnose anxiety.

He was not yet ready to call it fear.

But that's what he was: afraid, terrified that Elizabeth Ouvray was dying before his eyes, a little more every week, incrementally every session. He could not even be sure that his "treatment," his renowned methods of analysis, were helping to keep her alive. It was even possible that he was — mistakenly, unintentionally, horribly — speeding the painful process of her death.

At the beginning of the final month of his treatment of Elizabeth Ouvray, Dr. Paul Laner tried hypnosis for the first

time. It was not a mode of treatment he particularly con-
doned, believing as he did in the more conventional forms
of therapy. Indeed, he had to cram a quick "refresher
course" on hypnosis with a younger, more holistically-
inclined psychologist of his acquaintance.

"Let your scalp relax," he began the first time, using his
deepest, most soothing and mellifluous voice, and feeling
faintly ridiculous even saying the words. Elizabeth lay on
her back on the couch in the corner of his office, her skel-
etal hands folded over her stomach, her eyes closed.

He was seated beside her right shoulder.

"Allow even your hair to relax . . . relax your forehead,
feel your forehead grow smooth, smooth . . . relax your eye-
brows, eyelids, let your eyes fall back in your head, feel your
eyes relax, feel them relax . . . relax your cheekbones . . . your
lips, relax your tongue, let your jaw relax . . . relax the back of
your neck, and now your throat . . . feel how relaxed your
whole head is, your whole neck and throat . . . now let that
feeling of complete relaxation slide down your shoulders . . ."

When Elizabeth was visibly relaxed and breathing easily,
he led her through a series of non-threatening questions
and answers. Then he said, "Let's go further back now, Elizabeth, to a time when you were just a little girl. Now, while
you are absolutely safe and secure in the present, I will ask
you to go back to a time in your childhood when you were
afraid. Remember, Elizabeth, that whatever it was that
frightened you then, cannot hurt you now. The past is over.
It is safe for you to remember what frightened you. When I
count to three, you will remember something that frightened you when you were a little girl. One, two, three . . ."

"I'm in my bedroom," she said immediately.

Laner stared, surprised. This had the sound of something new, something previously uncovered.

119

"How old are you in this bedroom?"

"I don't know. Young. I'm really young."

"Look around the room, Elizabeth. What do you see?"

"Oh!" Suddenly, her voice was like a child's. "It's our first little apartment! I'm two."

Good grief, Laner thought, can this be true?

"Are you two years old?"

"Yes."

"Is it night time?"

"Yes."

"Your mother has put you to bed?"

"Yes."

"Are you alone in the bed?"

"No."

"No, Elizabeth?"

"Tubby."

"Your teddy bear is with you."

"Yes."

"And you feel . . . how do you feel?"

"Scared! I'm awake. I don't know why I'm awake. It's dark! Where's Mommy? Mommy? There's a noise! Mommy!"

Laner's own heart was beating rapidly, but he leaned forward to calm her.

"You are safe from the noise, Elizabeth, it cannot hurt you, I will not let it hurt you. Are you calling out for your mother?"

"Yes. No! I thought I was! But I'm not, I'm too scared, oh, what is that, who is that? *Mommy!*"

The last word burst from Elizabeth's throat as if it had broken loose from paralyzed vocal chords. She remained lying on the couch, but her head and shoulders strained upward, her eyes bulged beneath their lids, and she breathed in ragged gasps.

"It cannot hurt you, Elizabeth," Laner said, hoping he did not sound as unnerved as he felt. "Tell me what you see, tell me what it is that frightens you so."

"A face!" Elizabeth began sobbing, quick, keening sobs that sounded like a frightened child's. She was trembling all over, and his own hands were shaking. "He's got a flashlight. He's got curly hair. He's got a mean face, oh, it's the meanest face I ever saw! He's looking down at me, he's angry at me, he's going to hurt me!"

"Does he hurt you, Elizabeth?"

"Oh!" Her sobs caught in her throat, as if she were startled. "He's gone! Mommy's here and she's holding me . . . a burglar," she said next, in a wondering voice. "I can hear Mommy saying that. Shhh, Mommy says to me, it's all right, baby girl, it was just a dream, it was only a bad dream, that's all it was, forget all about it now, go back to sleep, it didn't happen, it never happened, it was only a bad dream . . ."

Soon after that, Laner brought Elizabeth up out of the hypnotic trance. She remembered nothing of what had transpired, so he told her.

"A *burglar?*" She was still as wide-eyed as a child. "That's where my nightmares came from? But my mother only meant to protect me."

"I'm sure that's true, Elizabeth."

"She told me it was only a dream . . ."

"And it became a recurring nightmare."

"Is that why I'm frightened of strangers, too?"

"What do you think, Elizabeth?"

She smiled tentatively. "I think maybe it is."

He thought maybe it was, too. In fact, he was positive of it. And he felt sure that now that Elizabeth had at last delved far enough into her subconscious to uncover the source of her fears, she would begin to recover.

But she did not.

She began to report horrifying nightmares.

At their next session, she reported a continued terror of strangers, along with her many other fears. Indeed, she looked as if she had slept even less that week than before. She reported that the headaches and muscle cramps that Laner suspected were a consequence of malnutrition had increased in frequency and intensity. He had been on the verge of hospitalizing her before; now he felt he surely must. But what an admission of failure on his part that would be! Still, how much worse it would be if she died when simple medical procedures like an IV might keep her alive.

The psychologist's own sleep was not much better than hers.

"She looks awful," he thought, "and what am I going to do now?"

He decided to hypnotize her again.

"All right," she said, dully.

Again, he relaxed her, although it took a long time, as he was anything but relaxed himself. Again, he led her through safe and easy memories, then back through the traumatic memory of the burglar, and then . . .

"Go further back now, Elizabeth, back as far as you can go to the first, the very first frightening thing that ever happened to you . . ."

"Please, I won't tell anyone!" she cried.

"What?" Laner was confused at the sudden and dramatic change in her voice and tone. "Where are you?"

"In my bedroom. Oh my God, please don't do that. I swear to you that I never told anyone, I won't tell anyone, I swear it."

122

"Elizabeth, how old are you?"

"Twenty-two."

What? Laner thought — twenty-two? But she was only nineteen in the present, in the here and now. What was going on?

"Where are you?" he asked again, trying to orient himself as much as to orient her.

"I'm sitting here on the edge of my bed, and I'm begging him, begging him . . ."

She began to sob convulsively.

"Begging him to do what, Elizabeth?"

"Begging him not to kill me. I won't tell anyone. I swear I won't. Please, please . . ."

She screamed, and Laner jumped back in his chair.

"Elizabeth," he said slowly, "who are you?"

"Susan Naylor," she whispered, "I am dying . . ."

Oh my God, he thought, my God, my God, what is this, what is this that is happening here?

This time when he brought her out of hypnosis, he did not tell her what she had said and done. He could hardly credit it himself. How could a 19-year-old patient suddenly "become" a different, even an older woman entirely? Could this possibly be an example of past-life regression such as he had read about (and disbelieved) in some medical journals? Could it be a form of ESP? If he wrote it up as such, he'd be laughed out of his practice. The psychologist sent her home, canceled all of his appointments for the rest of that day and secreted himself in a secluded recess of the medical library at a nearby hospital. For the rest of that afternoon, he read every case study he could locate that even slightly resembled the strange events that had transpired in his office.

He found no reassuring answers.

Near dinnertime, he called his wife.

"I'll be late," he told her. "I have to see a patient."

Elizabeth Ouvray lived in the second-floor rear apartment of a brick fourplex in a shabby neighborhood. It was twilight and getting cool outside by the time he rang her doorbell.

"Dr. Laner?" she said, when she saw him.

She was pale, exhausted-looking, shaking, and so was he.

"May I please come in, Elizabeth?"

"I'm . . ." She looked as if she were trying to come up with some good reason to turn him away. He suspected he was the first person to enter her apartment in a very long time. "I . . . all right . . . yes."

The doctor followed her into her living room, which was starkly furnished with furniture so nondescript it could have been rented. He sat down in the middle of her couch, but Elizabeth remained standing, propping herself against a wall as if it alone gave her the strength to remain upright.

"Elizabeth, today . . ."

"I don't want to know!"

"You're aware then, that something happened . . . something unusual . . . during hypnosis?"

"I think so . . . yes."

"Elizabeth, who is . . . was . . . Susan Naylor?"

The doctor held his breath, hoping she'd come up with some explanation, some conscious recognition of the name that would explain how a 22-year-old dead woman's memories got into Elizabeth Ouvray's brain.

She looked blank. "Who?"

He felt like crying. It wasn't only her life that was at stake here. His reputation, his 23-year counseling career, was about to go down the tubes because this insane young

124

woman had memories she had no logical reason for having!

"I'm sorry," she whispered.

Laner was appalled to realize he had actually spoken his thoughts aloud to her. He felt desperate enough to suggest, "I want to hypnotize you again, Elizabeth."

"Right here, Dr. Laner? You mean now?"

"Please," he said softly, gently. "Please."

She said she'd be most comfortable seated at the table in the kitchen, and so she led him there. She faced the chrome door of the refrigerator as he attempted one more time to relax her into a deep trance state. The contorted reflection he saw over her shoulders was of an old man who looked as if he had just been told that his favorite grandchild had been run over on her tricycle. The haggard woman reflected in the chrome bore little resemblance to the blonde beauty who'd walked through his office door at a time that now seemed so long ago.

When she appeared to be deep in trance, he made the hypnotic suggestion: "You are now Susan Naylor," and then he stood back to see what might happen next.

It was instantaneous.

"No!" she screamed, loud enough for the neighbors to hear. *"Please, no! Get away from me! Don't hurt me, I won't tell anyone! Please, don't hurt me, don't hurt me!"* She lurched to her feet, knocking the stool over, still screaming, *"No, no, no!"* When she turned toward the doctor, she was holding a butcher knife. *"Please don't kill me!"* she screamed — over and over, as she stabbed him in his throat.

When the police arrived at the urgent summons of several of the neighbors, they found Elizabeth, weeping and bloody, still holding the knife with which she had killed Dr.

Paul Laner. Her blouse was badly torn, revealing her ripped bra, and the zipper of her jeans was broken so that she had to hold it together with one hand.

"Tell us what happened," a detective, a woman, urged her. "Your neighbors reported hearing you scream for help."

"He was my psychologist," Elizabeth whispered. "I trusted him. And he came here tonight, and he tried to rape me. I'm so afraid all the time of everything, that's what he was treating me for, he knew how horribly afraid I am of men, and when he attacked me, *I . . . I . . .* killed him."

On the way to the hospital, she whispered to the policewoman, "Somebody told me that Dr. Laner got into trouble years ago with another female patient, but he was so good to me that I didn't believe it. Do you think it could be true?"

"It's true," the policewoman called her at the hospital to say. "At least *I* think it's true, although it was only a rumor at the time. It makes sense though, considering how obsessed even his wife and his colleagues admit that he was about you. What I've learned is that when he was just starting out, twenty-three years ago, there were rumors that he had an affair with a patient, supposedly as a part of her treatment, and that she had a child by him. Lousy bastard, abusing his power like that. They said she was blonde, like you, only 22 years old, and very beautiful."

"I'd like to hear her name," Elizabeth whispered.

"Naylor, Susan Naylor," the policewoman said, and then, because she heard Elizabeth moan, she added sharply, "What's the matter?"

"Nothing."

"There was a rumor that she was going to file a paternity suit," the policewoman continued, "but before that could happen she was murdered. Susan Naylor was stabbed one night by someone who broke into her apartment."

"Oh God," Elizabeth breathed. "They didn't catch him."

"Nope. They interrogated Laner, because of the rumors. But their only witness was the baby, Susan Naylor's two-year-old little girl. And the only word they got out of her was 'burglar.' Poor little thing. After her mother's murder, she was taken by her grandparents. Do you think Laner was her father? I'll bet you the bastard was, and I'll bet you he killed her mother to keep his precious reputation intact." The cop laughed. "At least, that's my wild theory, what do you think of it?"

"I think you're right," Elizabeth whispered.

"Well, you get to feeling better, okay?"

"I will now."

"What?"

"Bye."

"Bye."

The policewoman's hand lingered on the receiver after she hung up the phone. On her desk lay the old homicide file from which she'd been quoting to Elizabeth.

Elizabeth.

The child's name was Elizabeth.

"I think you're right," the policewoman whispered to herself. When no one was looking, she slid a few pages out of the file and slipped them into her morning newspaper, which she folded in half and dropped into her wastebasket.

We called him the Devil because he killed women at spiritual retreats: convents, mother houses, religious communes. Each victim was slain with an article of her faith: a rosary, in one case; a cross upon a deadly chain; a veil.

I was pulled into the case from an unusual angle when I got a call from an FBI field supervisor in Kansas City.

"Joseph Owen?" he inquired.

When I agreed that was me, he said, "We've got one, Joe."

"When was she killed?" I asked, holding my breath for the answer.

When he said, "Yesterday," I felt both relief and dread, because that was half of the answer I'd been waiting for since June.

"The victim was Lila Susan Pointe," he reported. "P-o-i-n-t-e. Twenty-seven years old. Caucasian. He strangled her with a white silk altar cloth from a chapel on the grounds of a religious retreat called Shekinah: S-h-e-k-i-n-a-h. I don't know what they're all about; it may be a cult. This murder fits the Devil's profile, Joe, except that we've got something nobody else has ever had: an eyewitness."

When I heard that, I pounded my fist on my desk, feeling exultant, like a kid saying, *yes!* It was the other half of the news I'd been waiting to hear.

"Our witness," he said, "is a woman he attacked but didn't kill because other people almost walked up on him.

128

That's the good news, from which you may infer bad. In addition to taking vows of poverty, obedience, and chastity, our witness added a vow of her own. Care to guess which one?"

When I didn't, he said, "Okay, I'll tell you: Our eyewitness took a five-year vow of silence . . . two years ago." His voice combined frustration with irony. "She won't say a goddamn word to any of us. I hear you're good at getting serial killers to chat, Joe. Would you come out and see if you can get her to talk?"

What he meant was that serial killers were my specialty within the FBI. More than two dozen of them had spilled their repellent guts to me. But I had never yet had the chance to talk to one of their victims, since up to now, they'd all been dead. For the first time, I had a live one.

I flew to Kansas City that morning.

For three years, the Devil had haunted the Midwest, striking seemingly at random, until a former priest within the FBI came to me with a hesitant theory.

"I've noticed," he said, "that the murders always fall on a saint's day associated with the Virgin Mother, or with other saints named Mary."

I would have laughed, because it was absurd, except that I knew the world of serial killers was like a cold, strange planet where each inhabitant lived according to his own weird logic. No doubt this one had an abusive mother named Mary, or Maria, or some damn thing. It was often that simple, and that nuts.

"Has the Devil ever killed in the month of June?" he asked me, and I told him no. "Has he killed in every other month?" he asked me, and I said yes.

"June," he said then, "is the only month in which there is

129

no saint's day for a Mary. July is also an exception because there are two celebrations on the same day, the sixteenth."

It was May when he told me his theory.

He and I waited anxiously through June and, sure enough, no murders were reported. Now, one death and a second attack had been reported for July sixteenth, right on schedule. If the ex-priest was right, I had to make our eyewitness break her vow of silence before July twenty-second, which would be the saint's day of Mary Magdalen.

It was six days away.

Before my flight, I said confidently to my wife, "She'll talk. Under these circumstances, only the devil himself would refuse to cooperate."

By that afternoon, July seventeenth, I was rocking over dirt and gravel in a rental car on a Missouri farm road south of Kansas City. The end of the line turned out to be a parking lot cut into the thick woods and situated in front of a long, low building constructed of redwood planks.

I stretched, working fifteen hundred miles of tension and stiffness out of my muscles. As my nostrils opened to let in more air, I smelled wood smoke. I heard the single human sound of wood being sawed and tasted the dust of a dry summer. Because I was an amateur horticulturist — a hobby I began because I wanted to pull something alive out of the earth, for a change, instead of dead and mutilated bodies — I could identify the trees around me: maples, pin oaks, sycamore, locust, and evergreens, rising to mature heights. Creeping vines filled the spaces between them.

I had a sense of people existing like squirrels, or termites — breathing, smelling, eating, sleeping in trees. In fact, I already had been informed that the members of this community called Shekinah did, indeed, inhabit simple lofts built

130

on stilts among the trees. At the moment, those private cabins were invisible to me; I could see only the headquarters building, which looked like a long, fallen redwood tree. I walked toward it, watching out for poison ivy and snakes, worrying about ticks.

Most signs of the police, sheriff's department, and FBI presence were gone, though very recently they would have been as thick on the ground as leaves. They'd had all the previous day and night and most of this day to gather their evidence, interview people — the ones who would talk — and remove the body. They'd be back, but for now I seemed to be the only investigative authority on the place. That suited me well, because I planned to make friends with this woman, our silent witness. It wouldn't help for her to see me as one more demanding man in an intrusive gang of pushy cops and agents.

Her name, I'd been told, was Sara.

I planned to come on to Sara quietly, respectfully, slowly.

I had it all figured out, down to the crucial moment when I would carefully slip my pen and notepad into my hands. Of course, she would talk to me. How could anyone refuse to talk if saying something would save a life? I marveled at how clumsy the cops who preceded me must have been to prolong her silence. I would put an end to that nonsense. She would talk, for me.

I was taken to a small, plain office occupied by a woman who appeared to be in her seventies. She was white-haired, lean, and tanned brown as a pecan. I thought she looked capable and strong in her commune uniform which consisted of forest-green trousers and a matching overshirt.

"I'm Joseph Owen," I told her, flashing my FBI identification.

"How do you do, Joseph Owen?" she said, smiling as easily as if nobody had been murdered in her little community. "I am what you might call the director of Shekinah, although my title, my *nom de spirit,* you might say, is Grandmother. They call me the GM when they think I can't hear them." Again she smiled, and her blue eyes twinkled. "If you think you can stand it, I invite you to call me Grandmother, too."

"I'll try," I said, and she laughed at the wry tone in my voice.

I knew her real name; in fact, I knew a fair amount about her and this commune, because I had taken time in Kansas City to copy and study the information a local field agent had put together, and I had all of that, plus copies of the police interviews, in my car. I knew, for instance, that Sara's vow of silence was total, allowing not even the sign language that is traditional with Trappist monks. She didn't write notes. She didn't nod, she didn't shake her head. In no way did she communicate.

"What's Shekinah?" I asked the GM, because the files were vague on that.

"It's a bona-fide religion," she replied, rather quickly.

"That's not what I meant," I said carefully. "But if you're suggesting the government can't make her talk because that would violate her religious freedom, of course you're right. However, I hope you won't fool yourself into thinking the government won't try to force her if they have to. They can make her silence a miserable and expensive experience for all of you."

"They?" she asked, making the point that I was one of them. "I'm afraid I have no talent for misery, Mr. Owen. And I will remind you that we already live under a vow of poverty."

132

I felt something like heartburn rise under my breastbone when she said all that, refuting my every point. I recognized the discomfort as frustration, not indigestion. Looking at her serene and contented face, I suddenly had the feeling it was going to become a familiar sensation in this case.

The GM walked me down a forest path that appeared unoccupied by humans until we looked up. Then we could see the lofts among the trees where members of the community lived alone. There was no indoor plumbing in the lofts, no electricity. Not because of their religious beliefs, she told me, but because it was cheaper that way.

"You want to know what we believe, Mr. Owen? We believe in the Ten Commandments, and that's all."

"Which of them forbids her to speak?" I asked.

The Grandmother stopped suddenly on the path and looked back at me. "That was very astute of you," she said, and I felt like a schoolboy who had guessed right on a test and pleased the teacher. "It is the ninth commandment from which Sara draws her will to silence."

I had to search my Sunday school memory to come up with it.

"Thou shalt not bear false witness, right? But nobody's asking her to lie."

"I'm afraid you do not fully understand the commandments, Mr. Owen, at least not as we do. We believe that personality is an illusion, a spider web of lies spun over the truth. We believe the true essence of every person is already perfect, forgiven, and saved. In regard to the ninth commandment, we believe that to say otherwise of any human being is to bear false witness against him."

"Or her," I suggested.

She smiled. "Those distinctions, too, are illusions."

"No original sin?" I asked.

"Only trite and unoriginal ones," she said, gently.

We had arrived at a wooden ladder where a rope hung down.

"Pull this," she instructed me, "and it will ring the bell in her cabin. Come see me afterwards if you wish."

I stopped her before she could walk away.

"You haven't said a word about the victim, Grandmother."

She stared off into the trees before she looked up at me again.

"Neither have you, Mr. Owen. The difference between us is that in my belief system, Lila Susan is no more dead than you and I are. It's you and the FBI who say she's dead, and who insist on finding her supposed killer. If you believe — really believe — in immortal life, as we do, you understand that no one can ever really die, and so nobody can possibly kill you."

As she walked calmly away and I pulled on the damn rope, I felt the heartburn rise again.

A trapdoor opened in the floor of the loft above me. I climbed the ladder, ten rungs hand over hand, and entered a Lilliputian chamber. There was a cot with a young woman seated on it, her back propped against the wood wall, her face turned down. There were books stacked against the walls, a basket of what looked like clean underwear under the cot, another basket with eating utensils, a small desk with a straight chair, a neat stack of towels, and a folded green uniform like the one she was wearing. Apart from four tall, ugly green plants in plastic pots, that was all there was in the square little room. Four windows provided cross ventilation; at one of them, the metal tubes of a wind chime

134

clinked in the breeze. I left the trapdoor open and sat beside it, cross-legged in my suit, on her wooden floor.

I felt hot, sweaty, itchy, but she looked cool.

"Sara? My name is Joe — Joseph Owen — and I'm an FBI agent. You must be sick of us by now, and I apologize very much for intruding on your privacy." I paused, carefully feeling my way into her silence. She had glanced up at me long enough for me to see a young, plain face with no makeup. All of the Devil's victims were young, in their twenties or late teens, many of them had brown hair, like hers, and several of them wore their hair pulled back from their face in a long ponytail, as this woman did. After a moment, I started in again. "I'm really sorry about what happened to your friend yesterday, and for what he put you through. We're all glad you survived!"

I let that thought lie between us for a moment while the wind chime played in the window. I was intimate with silence because my own mother had been a profoundly silent woman, except when she exploded in rage at something I — her only child — had done to prick the bubble of her silence. I knew how to wait it out, to coax and manipulate it. Because of my childhood, I hated silence, which was perhaps why I was so adept at getting stubborn people to talk to me.

"Sara, I don't want to frighten you, but the fact is, I'm here to protect you." Her body made an involuntary movement, and I had a feeling I had startled her, which was what I hoped to do in a sly way. I wanted to pull her off of her calm, silent pedestal, and to prod an exclamation out of her, even if it was only an Oh! or a No! If I could break the dam, force one word out of her compressed mouth, her vow would be irreversibly broken, and then she might as well tell me everything. I wanted to go slow, to win her trust, so

135

she'd do what I wished her to do, but there wasn't much time. I said, "If he thinks you can identify him, you're a threat to him, Sara. So I'm going to stick around to protect you."

That was her chance to indicate in some way that she hadn't seen his face, or that she couldn't really identify him, but she didn't do that. She just sat, not moving or speaking. I resisted an urge to shake her until her teeth rattled and words came tumbling out of her mouth. I wanted to tell her she was a spoiled brat, enjoying the luxury of a silence she could end at any time, but that her friend was not so fortunate. Lila Susan Pointe and the other victims were silent, too, but they would never open their mouths and speak to me.

"I'll be around, Sara," I promised her.

I descended from her loft, pulling the trapdoor shut behind me.

The truth was that she probably wasn't in any danger, because he had never killed between saint's days, and never in the same place on another day. The Devil was probably traveling toward his next victim, or even now stalking and studying her. But Sara didn't know that, and now I had an excuse for snaking my way into her life and her trust.

The GM offered me a sleeping bag and a commune uniform when I told her I was Sara's temporary bodyguard. The uniform was even more than I had hoped for; wearing that, I'd soon look as familiar to Sara as any member of her community.

In the GM's office, I said, "What are those ugly plants she grows?"

"They're milkweed, Joseph Owen. I imagine she grows them because they attract monarch butterflies."

Rather stupidly, I asked, "Why does she want to do that?"

The GM smiled. "Who wouldn't? Watch them sometime, Mr. Owen. You'll have the feeling of being in conversation with them. They don't appear to be afraid of us, they hang around as if they want to talk to us, as if they have something really important to tell us."

I tried to keep the cynicism out of my voice. "So she won't talk to people, but she talks to butterflies?"

The GM gently shrugged. "I don't know." She looked meaningfully into my eyes. "Milkweed itself is sensitive to disturbance. You can't jostle them or they'll die, or grow crooked."

"So what are you telling me?" I asked her. "That I shouldn't disturb Sara?"

Instead of answering me, she said, "Are you a reading man?"

"Do you count Clancy?" I asked her. "Koontz, King?"

"Of course." She smiled. "I think people who are readers are more likely to see symbolism where other people just see life."

"So you're saying I'm reading too much into milkweed and butterflies."

"I mean the truth has depth, but no layers."

"What the hell is that supposed to mean?"

The GM smiled at my annoyance. "It means you'll get nowhere by trying to peel the layers off her psyche."

"Jesus Christ!" The profanity exploded from my mouth into the peaceful atmosphere. The entire law enforcement community was seriously annoyed with these people, and I was especially irritated by the sight of the smug old lady standing so serenely in front of me. "There has been a murder. Of one of your own people. And she won't talk, and you talk in goddamn riddles instead of really cooperating. You are selfish, infuriating people."

I was a lot more startled by my outburst than she appeared to be.

"I apologize," I said, and tried to put a rueful, charming smile on my face. "Obviously I am a rude and frustrated man."

She smiled, kindly. "Think nothing of it."

I berated myself all the way back down the path into the woods, where I changed clothes behind a tree and spread out my borrowed sleeping bag to sit on while I waited for Sara to make her first descent from the loft. I was tired, and under time pressure, but that was no excuse. I was going to have to get myself under professional control, or I'd blow it and scare her away.

Day after day I followed Sara like her shadow, and every night I slept under her loft, sometimes staring up at the floor of it in utter frustration.

She wouldn't talk; she wouldn't damn talk.

But I talked, chattering like a friendly magpie, sometimes about serial killers in general, sometimes about the Devil in particular, frequently about the heartrending stories of his victims and their families.

And nothing moved her to speak.

On our way to the latrines, with me shuffling behind her in the leaves, I said, "He has already killed a lot of women, Sara. We know his pattern. The next time he will strike is only five days from now."

Her job at the commune was janitorial work, so I grabbed a sponge and scrubbed floors right beside her. While we worked, I said, "I don't know how much you know about serial killers, Sara, but they come in two types:

the disorganized kind and the organized kind. Our guy is the latter. He's very organized, very clever, very careful. He scouts out his locations and studies his victims before he makes his attack."

Sitting beside her at the communal dinner table, I whispered, "A place like this, Sara, all he has to do is hide in the woods and watch and wait for his chance."

Going to chapel at sunrise, I said, "We think we know how he gets into some of the places, Sara. He arrives as a repairman, or a deliveryman, which is the only possible way he could worm himself into convents, for instance."

In the evenings, because she didn't object, I climbed her ladder and propped myself on the floor beside a milkweed pot, and I carried on a one-sided conversation with her. "As far as we know, you're the only person who can identify him, Sara. An artist could draw a portrait from your description, but we don't want too much time to go by or you might begin to forget what he looked like. We could broadcast the picture, pass it out to places like this, so they can protect their members. We can find him, Sara, with your description. You can save lives."

Once, I said, "It's you and me and God against the Devil, Sara."

As Monday passed, then Tuesday, Wednesday, Thursday, it became more difficult for me to be gentle and patient with her. I thought she was ridiculous, a fool playing an egotistical, dangerous game with other women's lives.

I asked the GM, "Why silence?"

Her answer was to hand me a cassette tape, which I took out to the parking lot where I could listen to it privately in my rental car.

The voice that emerged from the car's dashboard was

light, girlish, and a little breathless, as if she were nervous, or as if she'd been running and had only stopped long enough to drop a few thoughts into a tape recorder:

"This is Sara," the voice on the tape announced self-consciously. It felt strange to finally hear the voice that went with the silent face I'd been studying so closely. The words tumbled out so fast I had to reverse the tape several times to understand them.

"This is Sara. I've said enough in my life. Way too much. Lots of things that hurt people. Things that make me feel awful, just knowing I said them. I'm good at saying all the wrong things. Mean things. Lies. I talk all the time, too. I lie like a rug, I lie like a whole carpet store! I can't stop it, I don't know how to stop lying, except to stop speaking altogether. I drive people crazy with my talking and lies. They can't trust me, they tell me so. Nobody should ever trust anything I ever say! I'm boring, I'm self-centered, I never listen to anybody, and I know that, and the words keep coming, all the same. I'm sick of the sound of my own voice! I'm going to stop talking, because all I ever do when I open my mouth is lie and hurt people. So, I'm going to start listening. I'm not going to say anything, not anything, unless God puts the words in my mouth. Starting now. Right now. This is the last word. Honest."

The next sound on the tape was her giggling, and then she said once more, and dramatically: "Starting . . . now!"

There was nothing more on the tape.

I sat in the car, thinking the amazing thing was that she'd done it, for two years, so far. Amazing.

In the GM's office, I handed back the tape and said, "So what did she lie about that hurt people so much?"

"It wasn't anything big," the GM told me, "nothing like falsely accusing a man of rape or murder, for instance. Just a constant stream of little lies, gossipy, vicious little fabrications that hurt people's feelings more than anything. She was disliked as a consequence. Now she's quietly accepted everywhere she goes in the community."

"Like a house plant," I said drily. "What does she get out of it?"

"Relief, I think," the GM replied. "She used to steal things, too. Clothing, mostly, which she would wear in front of all of us and claim it was hers. Blatant, outright lies, looking you straight in the face."

"Does she still steal things?"

"No, that stopped soon after she went silent."

"So it's working, her silence?"

"I don't know," the GM admitted. "There's no way for me to know if she has finally learned to tell the truth to herself."

On Saturday, one day before the saint's day for Mary Magdalen, I confronted the GM in her office. "She's lying to herself," I said, "if she thinks she's doing the right thing this time."

"But Mr. Owen, if she talked to you, how would you know she was telling the truth? Have you thought about that? What kind of witness would she make in court, a self-confessed, nearly pathological liar?"

"I don't care what she does in a courtroom." Suddenly, I was angry again and yelling at the old woman. "I just want her to tell me enough to stop him! Don't you get it? He's going to kill another woman . . . tomorrow . . . and another and another after that, unless Sara identifies him. When we catch him, we'll gather other evidence, so we won't even need her for a conviction, but right now, she's got to talk. If she doesn't talk by tomorrow morning, she'll have a lot more than lies on her conscience."

141

The GM smiled patiently at me, as a grandmother might at a toddler having a tantrum, and she merely said, "Well, she might even lie about his appearance, you know."

I felt like strangling both of them.

I didn't sleep that night in my bag under the god-damned loft, because I felt haunted by the ghosts of the other women he'd killed, all of them urging me to *do* something before other women joined their dreadful sorority.

Sunday, July twenty-second, passed in silence, with me dogging Sara's footsteps as usual, but for once I remained as silent as she. That night the telephone brought word of what I feared most: The Devil had struck on schedule, killing a woman at a Buddhist retreat north of San Francisco.

I stalked on stiff legs to Sara's cabin and climbed the ladder, clumsy in my fury and sorrow.

"Well, you've done it," I told her, my voice as cold as the sound of the metal wind chimes. "You've let him kill another one."

I gave her the details, all of them, sparing her nothing.

If she had a reaction, I couldn't see it in the dark cabin where she sat on her cot, her back turned toward me, her face to the wall.

That night, I raged over the phone to the field supervisor.

"I hate these people," I told him. "They don't give a damn about the victims, and I don't give a damn about them."

The supervisor laughed, but it was a cynical sound of understanding, rather than amusement. "So, Joe . . . no more Mr. Nice Guy?"

"Hide and watch," I advised him.

The next day, methodically, I set about turning the other members of the community against her. I took them aside individually and in little groups under the pretext of interviewing them one more time, and I spoke to them of the suffering of the victims, the heartbreak of the families, and of their own potential for becoming a next victim. I played on their compassion, their fear. I allowed them to get a glimpse of my frustration, of my decent motives, of my anxiety, and of how terrible I felt over my failure to get Sara to talk. By the time I finished with them, I had them looking over their shoulders for fear the Devil was hiding in the woods, watching, waiting, looking them over, winnowing them out, selecting his next victim from among all of them.

One by one, they responded as I hoped they would, in frightened or indignant or sympathetic words. They said, "I'll talk to Sara!" or . . . "Sara has to break her silence!" or . . . "It's not right, what she's doing, it's not holy!" One of them even said to me, "Sara is being selfish and wicked, and I'm going to tell her so."

For the first time, then, I left the commune.

For twenty-four hours I stayed away, luxuriating in a motel while I allowed my poison to do its work.

When I returned, the GM met me at the headquarters door.

She said, "What have you done, Joseph Owen?"

Instantly, I felt triumphant.

"Is she talking?" I asked.

"No." But the GM looked worried for the first time since I'd met her. "You'd better see her. She's in her cabin."

I hurried down the path, feeling exultant.

At first, when I stepped inside the cabin, I didn't think she was there.

"Sara?" I called, which was silly, because there was hardly anything left in the cabin except her cot. The milkweed pots were gone. The blankets and sheets had been pulled off the cot and pushed under it. The baskets of underwear and eating utensils were gone. So was the stack of towels, and the books.

Dammit! Had she run away from me?

I felt shocked by the rage and disappointment.

But then I saw a movement in the jumble of bedclothes under the cot and I realized Sara was wrapped up in them. She had crawled under her cot and covered herself from toe to head in the sheets and blankets.

I heard a muffled sound, and thought at first it was a bird.

Then I realized she was weeping, unable for once to control the sound of her own voice.

My thought was savage: *Good!*

But now I could afford to be gentle, now I could play the good cop once again. I knelt down near her and said softly, "Sara? When you're ready to talk to me, I'll be right here. I won't ever leave you, Sara, not until you're ready for me. I'll be here for you when the time comes."

I slept in her cabin that night, instead of underneath it.

There came a point, however, when my own nature silently called, and I had to descend the ladder to find a john. I took the opportunity to make a fast trip to retrieve the sleeping bag from the GM's office. Sara was going to talk that night, I knew it, and if she didn't I was going to lock the trapdoor if I had to and keep her a prisoner in her cabin until she did what I wanted her to do.

The GM walked in as I was leaving her office with the bedroll.

Once again her face was unlined, her smile pacific.

"Aren't you worried anymore?" I asked her. "You seemed worried earlier."

"Prayer is a marvelous antidote to worry, Mr. Owen."

"You could probably force me to go away," I told her.

"This is Sara's opportunity for growth," was her calm reply.

"If I were Sara," I said, and I actually laughed, "I think I'd shoot you."

"That, too," said the Grandmother, smiling, "would offer enormous spiritual opportunities for her."

But this time, I was determined to have the last word.

"Your other members don't seem quite as convinced as you are that they're immortal. I get the feeling they're afraid to die."

I was astonished to see tears appear in the GM's blue eyes.

"Thank you, Joseph," she said, "for giving all of us a chance to face our own worst fears."

Damn the woman, she left me speechless, as usual.

I brushed past her, but she surprised me again by putting a hand on my arm to stop me. "Mr. Owen, tell me again about the pattern of organized serial killers, will you?"

I did it quickly, because I was in a hurry to resume my vigil over Sara, so she wouldn't try to escape while I was gone.

"They are methodical, careful, clever," I recited. "They study their victims, who are often very similar to each other, so as to know the best time and means of approach and attack. Frequently, they win their victim's trust by coming on as friendly and sincere, or in need of help. Often, once they have their victims, they hold them prisoner for some time, toying with them, before actually killing them."

"I see," the GM said, and her blue eyes looked brightly into mine. "Are you a good listener, Mr. Owen?"

"Of course," I said, curtly. "That's my business."

"Good," was all she said before releasing me.

I hurried back down the path thinking, what the hell was that all about?

The next saint's day on which the Devil would strike would not come until September, so there was a little time for us, but probably not for me. There was no way the higher-ups would let me stay out in the boonies trying to pressure just one witness. I figured I had only a little more time left before they called me back to my other work. But I would make the most of every minute of the time I had with Sara, if I had to tie her to her cot and show her photographs of the Devil's victims to make her finally talk to me.

It was a hot July, and the air was thick with humidity.

I heard a sound in front of me and realized it was Sara's trapdoor opening.

No! I thought, she's not getting out of there, I'm not letting her leave that cabin until she talks!

I ran forward, through the trees, nearing the stilts on which her home was built just as she kicked the ladder away.

Hell! She couldn't defeat me that way, I'd just prop the ladder up again! I slowed my pace, laughing at her for thinking she could keep me away from her.

And then I saw her feet and her legs drop through the hole.

I expected her to drop on down to the ground.

Instead, her legs dangled through the opening; her body knocked against the edges of the hole.

"Sara!"

With a sudden, horrible realization, I comprehended

146

what she had done. I stumbled toward her, yelling her name. Reaching her legs, I embraced them, and lifted them, so that her full weight couldn't fall downward. Above me, through the hole, I saw that she had tied her sheets together, tied one end over the beam in her cabin, and circled the other end around her neck. Then she had jumped through the hole in the floor.

I shouted desperately for help.

Members of the community came running. Two of them got into her cabin through the windows. They untied her and lowered her gently into our waiting arms. We laid her on the ground in the leaves.

"Sara?" I whispered to the still and silent face.

She had tried to hang herself.

Was she still alive?

Had her neck been broken as she fell through the floor?

After a moment, Sara's eyelids quivered and she moaned, the most beautiful sound I had ever heard.

When I was sure she would live, I ran to find the Grandmother.

After that, I simply walked to my rental car and drove away.

My hands trembled on the steering wheel because the Devil was still out there and I knew him well. I glanced in the rearview mirror and saw a white-faced man. My foot shook on the accelerator as I thought about my reputation for understanding serial killers. Again, I glanced in the mirror. Oh yes, I knew them as well as I knew myself.

I had studied her and stalked her, imprisoned her, tortured her by my presence and my demands, and I had nearly killed her.

And she was only the latest of my victims.

On my flight home, I mentally reviewed the names of the

men who were dead because of my investigations, men who were, in many ways, all alike. They'd been killed upon capture, or by the death penalty. They, too, I had stalked and studied, before snatching them and imprisoning them until they were put to death.

I went home to my wife — but then, many organized types of serial killers are married, or have girlfriends. I was no different.

I was no different.

The Devil was apprehended within the year, but I was gone from law enforcement by then, having quit in order to use my law degree in ways that would not tempt me to become what I hated. Somebody had to catch the killers, but it didn't have to be me.

I do a lot of gardening now.

I'm very familiar with milkweed and monarchs.

Three years after I left Shekinah, I received a letter from the Grandmother.

"Dear Joseph Owen," the letter began, in her own unmistakable style. "I thought you would want to know that Sara has recovered beautifully, with no ill effects. She is talking now, rather like a baby with her first words. Her voice sounds rough from lack of use, and she is shy about what she says and to whom she speaks. I do believe she accomplished what she set out to do: to learn to love the truth, and to speak only that, as best she can. The world is, I believe, a sweeter place as a consequence. Frequently I hear her laugh, a welcome and lovely sound to me.

"She told me she desperately wanted to speak to you when you were here, but that she could feel lies building up inside her mouth, and she was terrified that if she spoke she would lead you in such wrong directions you would never catch your killer, and many other women might die. She remained silent to save their lives. Then she tried to kill herself in order to make sure she could not harm you or any woman by speaking the lies that were tempting her.

"Now Sara dreams of the women whom you speak of as being killed, and they talk to her and tell her they are alive in spirit.

"I hope this will comfort you, Joseph Owen."

I threw away the letter, but not in anger.

I've thrown away my scrapbooks, too, the ones I used to keep on the serial killers I helped to stalk, imprison, and kill. Like Sara, I've learned to tell the truth to myself. And so, I no longer allow myself to keep trophies of my victims.

IT HAD TO BE YOU

I've kept this secret for years, but I'm telling it now: My sister, Crystal, was possibly the first person to see Marilyn Monroe's image appear on Mount Rushmore.

Remember that incredible week?

You *don't* remember, do you?

It's the strangest thing, how I seem to be the only person in America who remembers. It's as if we suffer national amnesia. Ask any American, "Do you remember when Marilyn Monroe appeared on Mount Rushmore?" and they'll laugh at you, and say, "Are you crazy? That's a tabloid story, like Bigfoot and Nessie. I suppose you believe in *them,* too?"

Americans don't seem to comprehend that the story of Marilyn Monroe on Rushmore is only treated like a tabloid fabrication *here;* in other parts of the world, people remember it as the actual, astonishing event it really was. Their media run "Marilyn Retrospectives" every year on the anniversary of her appearance. In Japan, she's nearly a religious icon. Believe me, *she's* the reason — not the Presidents — why thousands of foreign tourists stream into South Dakota, like pilgrims to Lourdes.

Americans think they're fools, those Marilyn-worshiping foreigners, but they're fools with money. We're delighted to sell them little Indian tom-toms (made in Korea) to take back home to their kiddies, but they search in vain for souvenirs of MM on Rushmore. They come, in their rented cars and tour buses, hoping to find photographs and commemorative books and souvenir paperweights so they can hold her in their hands, along with George, Tom, Abe, and Teddy, but all they ever find are the presidents. They don't find any record of her appearance at Rushmore. You know that's true, if you've ever been there. Think about it: Have you ever seen any Marilyn souvenirs sold in the "trading posts" beneath the monument?

No, the event has vanished from *our* national memory, just as she eventually vanished from the face of the mountain.

But I'm telling you — I'm *reminding* you — she was there! For that all-too-brief but magical week, *she* was there. I really do think my sister saw her first, so it's possible I saw her second. But I'm getting ahead of myself.

I remember it all, even if nobody else in this country does.

It took us a couple of endless days to drive from Kansas City, Missouri, to the campground on a pine-forested ridge east of Mount Rushmore: two sweltering, interminable days of driving through Missouri, Nebraska, and South Dakota in ninety-degree heat without air conditioning, and one night in a tacky motel, with Mom and Dad either arguing or not speaking to each other most of the time.

In the car, Crystal and I ate the peanut butter and cracker "sandwiches" that Mom had packed, and drank lukewarm water from the Thermos — because Mom thought Cokes gave me pimples — and sang as many popular songs as we could remember the words to, and stared out the windows of the back seat of the Chevy the rest of the time.

Crystal looked miserable, and I was bored out of my skull and wondering how we were all going to be able to stand being cooped up together for two whole weeks on the road.

151

I had recently earned my driver's license, and my parents had promised to turn the wheel over to me now and then, once we got out of the heaviest of the summer tourist traffic. But that hadn't happened yet; it seemed as if the entire southern half of America was driving toward the northern half of it. So I was stuck in the back seat with my ten-year-old sister. Our ultimate destination on that year's vacation trip was supposed to be Dad's sister's family in Seattle.

We never made it past Mount Rushmore.

The morning when Marilyn Monroe began to appear on the monument, Mom and Dad woke up fighting, before dawn's early light, even. Maybe they'd never slept, it's entirely possible that they only held it down — the noise and the nasty words — during the night to enable Crys and me to sleep, and then as soon as they heard me slip out to the campground bathroom, they started in again, lying there in their separate bedrolls on the canvas floor of our tent. They probably figured Crystal would sleep through their furious whispering, where I wouldn't. They knew that if they woke me up, I'd fly out of the tent and run off into the night, and they were scared of that possibility, especially now that I could drive by myself.

I had run off once before, on a family camping trip to the Lake of the Ozarks just three weeks earlier. It had scared them both half to death when they couldn't locate me for several hours — they thought I'd drowned, or some hillbilly had captured me — and it made them start to look with wary eyes at me if I was in the room when they would start to argue, after that. (I'd been perfectly safe the whole time I was gone, having stumbled down a country road to the highway, where I sat on the stoop of a Dairy Queen in the sun for hours, getting a tan and flirting with the boys who drove in for burgers or Cokes. I got burned from the sun and also got poison ivy from my furious plunge through the thick Ozark foliage surrounding our tent, but it was worth it.)

So it wasn't as if they didn't love us, or ever think about us.

They did, but they got distracted by their own heat and noise. What did they fight about? What time to get up in the morning, where to eat breakfast, what to eat for breakfast, when to stop for bathrooms, which road to follow on the map . . . and private things, in angry whispers in their bed and bedrolls, things I absolutely did not want to overhear.

This time, however, it was Crystal who ran away, only she was a quiet little thing who just slipped out without them even noticing at first. None of us knew she was gone.

As I said, I was off in the campground ladies room, getting a shower before the hordes of other women and girls trooped in, holding their toothbrushes aloft like flags to stake their claim to their places in line for the showers. It was worth forcing myself to roust before sunup, just to have the bathroom to myself.

Basically, I hated camping, I hated being on vacation with my parents, and I hated them. Well, what can I say, I was sixteen. I loved my little sister, though, and had long considered it my job to shelter her from the acrimony between our parents. I didn't want her to feel as bad about it as I had during those five years before she came along to keep me company in the misery.

After Crystal was born, it was easier for me to tell Mom and Dad to shut up — or run away from them — because then I had somebody besides myself to do it for, to protect. I felt guilty about leaving Crystal behind that time in the Ozarks when I ran away, but it had seemed at the time as if everything was closing in on me, even my responsibility toward her, when all I really wanted was to be left back home, on my own with my friends, in Kansas City.

As of that summer, I was even beginning to resent Crystal — how much I thought she needed me — and to feel guilty about feeling that way, and naturally I hated *those* feelings, too. I was a mess of self-pity and self-righteousness, and Marilyn healed me, and not only me.

What I'm telling you, this story, I've adapted from the diary (we'd call it a journal now, I suppose) which I kept on that trip. If at times I sound a bit young in the telling, it's because I was, then. We were all younger then, we Americans. Perhaps that's why it's hard for people to recall, because children change and grow, but they don't always remember the moment, the place, or the reason.

I kicked rocks coming back from the bathroom, feeling fresh as the piney air around me. Ten steps from the flap of the tent, I heard *them* arguing, and I seriously considered not going back in. But I stuck my head in anyway, kind of to see what they'd do, and sure enough, Mom and Dad looked at my face, then looked at each other, and then silently turned their backs and pretended to return to sleep. I felt suddenly, pleasantly, powerful, because my mere presence was enough to silence them.

Crystal's bedroll was empty.

"Where's Crys?"

"Bathroom," Mom said, sounding muffled by bedding.

I knew that wasn't true, or I'd have seen her myself. It was just barely light out, and I didn't like the idea of a ten-year-old girl wandering around the campground alone in the almost-dark. I also felt suddenly afraid that she'd picked up from me the idea of running away.

★ ★ ★ ★ ★

When I found Crys, she was sitting on a huge rock on the ridge overlooking the Black Hills and the monument and the valley below. We'd arrived late the night before, so we hadn't seen anything but the campground yet. I was really relieved to find her. She was staring — her knees drawn up to her chin, her arms hooked around them — spellbound into the distance.

I came up behind her and crawled onto the rock to sit beside her.

It was pretty impressive, the sight of those four huge faces.

The first thing I said to Crystal was, "Do you think Thomas Jefferson can hear Mom and Dad yelling at each other?" I wanted to let her know she wasn't alone in her distress, and I wanted to make her laugh.

"They woke me up," she said. "I wanted to scream at them."

"I know."

"Who's the other one?"

"The other one?" On the mountain, she meant. "Well, to our far left, that's George Washington, and of course you know he was our first President . . ."

"We already studied him," she agreed, impatiently.

"And next to him is Thomas Jefferson, and then there's Theodore Roosevelt, and the one on our right is Abraham Lincoln." I wanted to be either a writer or a history teacher when I grew up, which is why I was keeping a diary, and why I frequently took it upon myself to read travel books about the places we visited, and then to educate my little sister. "The sculptor was a man named Gutzon Borglum. He worked on them from 1927 until he died in 1941. Originally, he was going to carve them down to their waists, but

155

he died before he could do all that. The heads, alone, though, are sixty feet high! And the reason they look so real, like they're looking right at you, is that the pupils of their eyes are actually these three-foot long posts carved out of the granite, and —"

"Who's the *other* one?"

"The other one?"

"Her! I never knew we had a woman president. Who is she?"

"What are you talking about, Crystal?"

And then I saw it: a faint outline on the mountain just to the left of George Washington, in the blank space where the sculptor had originally planned for Roosevelt to be. Only it wasn't blank. I could just barely see it at first, but even so, it was most definitely an outline of a female form. Most definitely. Not just a head, either, but a whole body, down through the spaghetti straps, the tight bodice and skirt of her dress, to the high-heel shoes. High-heel shoes? The outline was getting darker, too, as the rising sun shone fuller and fuller about it. Upon her. Now it looked like an etching. Now it was filling in, like an Etch-A-Sketch, so we could begin to see how bouffant her hair was, how wide her eyes, how full her lips, how round her curves. It wasn't a sculpture, like the presidents, but more like a painting in stone.

"Oh, my God," I whispered, and then I jumped up on the boulder, nearly losing my balance in my excitement. "Oh, my God! Crystal, this is impossible, but that's Marilyn Monroe!"

"Be careful!" Crys yelled at me, and pulled at the bottom edge of my shorts, trying to get me to sit down with her again. "What's going on? I'm getting scared! You're scaring me! What's happening? Who's Marilyn Monroe?!"

"It's a miracle!" I shouted to the valley.

Mom and Dad didn't think it was a miracle, when we dragged them out of the tent — away from an argument over whether or not the milk in the cooler was still fresh enough to pour over cereal — and out to the ledge. We wouldn't tell them why we were pleading and begging and insisting, because we knew they wouldn't believe us, not until they saw her themselves.

Once Mom recovered from her first astonishment, she said, "It's a trick of light."

But Dad's opinion was, "No, somebody's projecting it from somewhere in back of us, from an airplane, maybe. It's an advertising gimmick."

Crys and I turned to look up at the pale blue sky, but it was empty of everything including clouds.

"Oh, please," Mom was scathing, and didn't even bother to look. "An airplane? How about a flying saucer, while you're at it? What airplane could hold an image still for so long?"

"A helicopter," he retorted. "A Harrier jet."

"Oh, stop. It's a trick of light, that's all."

Before they could really get into arguing about *that*, I said in a hurry, "Let's get in the car and get closer! Let's see if we can still see her from any direction! Please?" I was, myself, determined to go chasing that image if I had to steal the keys from my mother's purse, and take off with Crystal and the car.

"It's only an advertising gimmick," Dad grumbled.

But he was curious enough to indulge us, and so we all ran back and piled into the car and started driving around the area. We found out that she was, indeed, visible from any angle, and from anywhere you could see the monument. Uphill, downhill, there she was; daybreak, noontime, and twilight, there she still was!

As each amazing hour passed, and more and more people noticed her, her image became clearer and clearer upon the mountain, until there was no longer any chance of anybody denying that she was there. There was one time of day when George Washington's face cast a shadow that covered her face, but you still couldn't miss the hair, or the rest of her body. She was more than five hundred feet tall, for heaven's sake! Her voluptuous figure was turned slightly toward the presidents, but the full and radiant incandescence of her smile was directed toward the land below the monument, where all of us were staring back up at her.

She was there all that first night, too, in the lights which came on every evening to illuminate the presidents. In the spotlights, her tight, spaghetti-strap dress sparkled like sequins.

Crystal and I squatted on our rock, like Indians, for hours in the darkness, until Mom came out and put her foot down, insisting we come into the tent and go to bed. We could hardly bear to wait until morning, to see if *she* was still there.

And that was the first day.

The second day of Marilyn Monroe's presence on Mount Rushmore was the beginning of pandemonium. When people woke up and looked outside their travel trailers and their motel rooms and their tents, like us, and realized her image was still smiling down at them from beside George Washington, they went nuts.

We drove right into town, or what I called "town," although it was really just the big area of parking lots and "trading posts" and information centers for the monument, and hung around there all day, where the action was. Before you could say "Good Morning, America," the television network news shows had crews landing at the airports at Rapid City and Sioux Falls, and then helicoptering out to the monument. Soon, it seemed as if every single one of us tourists from out of state got interviewed at least once by some reporter from some rinky-dink station or newspaper from somewhere in the country. By late afternoon, the international media was on the scene, too, until you could hardly hear yourself think for the whup-whup of helicopters dipping and twirling all around the monument and the parking lots, trying for the best photographic angle.

And you wouldn't have believed how fast some folks could set up a booth to sell "Marilyn Monroe on Mt. Rushmore" T-shirts! That was just the beginning, too. Dad joked that there must have been five factories in Taiwan, just waiting to get the word to put a rush on Monroe salt-and-pepper shakers and little ceramic statues of her with the wind blowing her skirt up, and copies of that nude calendar photograph of her, you know the one. But all of that came later in the week, most of it arriving at the worst possible time, as things turned out.

In the meantime, on that second day — when we were supposed to be well on the road to Seattle — Crystal and I wandered around on our own. We kept walking on the heels and stumbling into the backs of people who would be walking normally in front of us one minute, and then stopped dead on the sidewalk the next minute, staring up at *her*, as if they'd all at once been turned to stone, themselves.

Crys and I got to giggling about all the open mouths and wide eyes, until we had to lean against a stranger's Toyota and laugh until we were crying. We pleaded with each other, as we each kept making jokes about it, to "Stop, oh, please, stop!"

Too late, I realized the Toyota was occupied, only the owner wasn't inside the car, she was seated, cross-legged on its hood. I quickly pulled Crystal to her feet, and both of us moved away from the vehicle.

The woman on the hood, who was pretty obviously a Native American, was staring back at us.

"Some kind of religious hysteria?" she asked me.

"What?" I didn't know what she meant. She looked quite a bit older than I was, but younger than Mom. She had been wordlessly sitting up there — her black hair hanging way down her back and her bold nose pointed toward the monument — like a hood ornament. Now the dark Indian eyes that had been looking at *her* were observing the antics of my sister and me.

"It's a sacred mountain," she said, and pointed with her right arm to the monument. "We've been trying to tell white people that for centuries. So I guess it figures that a goddess would appear on it. I just never guessed it would be one of *yours.*" She laughed in a way that managed to sound indignant, sad, and amused all at once. She didn't seem to be upset that we'd leaned on her car, however, so I tugged Crystal a little closer to the front of it, so we could hear her better. I didn't know how she could stand sitting on the hot metal, until I saw she had a plaid blanket under her.

"We Lakota believe the entire range of hills is our sacred mother from whom comes our food and our shelter," she said then, speaking directly to Crystal, who was clinging to me and looking shy. "Or, at least, it used to provide all that, until you guys took it away from us." She said it with more resignation in her voice than rancor, but I looked down at the ground, feeling vaguely guilty, anyway. But then she commanded my attention again by saying, "Look, you can see the shape of her in the line of the hills.

She's lying down. There is her head —"

"I see her shoulders!" Crys let go of me and jumped up and down, thrilled. I understood that we weren't talking about Marilyn now, but rather about a much, much older — even ancient — female spirit that Native Americans attributed to the Black Hills.

"There's the curve of her bosom." The Indian woman pointed, and I thought that I saw it. "The mounds of her belly and her hips."

"I see her legs!" Crys looked up at me. "Do you see?"

I saw the dark, reclining form, all right, of a woman lying on her side, gazing our way. She was a lot bigger than Marilyn's image, because she was the profile of all the hills put together, and she was horizontal, where Marilyn was — for once, as my own father had joked — vertical.

"These hills are womanly," the woman on the car told us.

I thought I could actually feel the Black Hills at that moment, and they felt like a cool embrace on that hot day. I imagined I could feel the pull and attraction of them, and I remembered the way my eyes couldn't stop looking at them when we were driving toward them, the way I couldn't turn away for very long and look at anything else, and the desire that was getting stronger and stronger in me to get as close to them as I could, to walk into that mysterious darkness and let it enfold me. I thought I smelled something in the hot summer air — part baby powder, part some yeasty doughy aroma like bread cooking, part Shalimar perfume, part evergreen, and also something that smelled like my own body, and made me feel embarrassed and excited all at the same time.

Whether it was Marilyn I was smelling, or the sacred mountain mother, or the real live Indian woman beside us, or my own hot, sweaty self, I couldn't tell. Everything was getting confused in my mind as the woman talked to us, and I was beginning to have a hard time telling what was real.

It was real, all of it. And it was unreal, too.

Beside me, Crystal whispered, "Can we go up there?"

The Native American woman and I looked at each other.

"It is a miracle, isn't it?" I said.

She shrugged. "It's a sacred mountain. I'll say this for her: At least she just appeared on it without hurting it; she didn't carve herself into the very flesh of our mother."

"But what about Crazy Horse, down the road?" Crys asked her.

I thought it took some guts for Crystal to ask the Indian woman about that sculpture-in-progress, seventeen miles to the southwest. What Crys meant was: If it's not okay to carve a president into the mountain, why is it okay to carve an Indian chief?

"He never wanted an image to be made of him," the woman told us. "He wouldn't allow paintings or photographs while he was alive."

So it was *not* all right, she was telling us.

But I got the distinct impression that having Marilyn on the mountain was okay, even with her.

That night, the evening of the second day, the story was broadcast all over the world, and front-page photographs displayed the image to millions of people, some of whom believed it was true, and some of whom didn't.

Some of the ones who didn't began to arrive on the third day.

But so did hundreds, thousands, of the ones who did — and that's when the healings began.

The morning of the third day dawned quiet in our tent.

At the time, I didn't recognize that as an early sign that something fantastic was about to happen — a phenomenon that would be even more amazing than an image of a dead movie star appearing on a national monument.

After Crys and I had returned from checking out the view from the ridge (*she* was still there, and her smile competed with the sun, for wattage), for our breakfast of cereal in plastic bowls, we found Mom and Dad not speaking to each other while they were drinking their plastic cups of coffee. But it was a different kind of not-speaking, a kind that seemed peaceful and relaxed, for a change. I held my breath, waiting for the first word of dispute between them.

"More coffee, hon?" my father asked her.

"No, thanks, sweetie," Mom replied, smiling at him.

Crys and I exchanged glances. *Hon? Sweetie?*

"Don't you want some cereal?" Mom asked him.

"No, I think I'll wait for lunch."

I saw Crystal clench her jaw. Here's where it would start, the sarcastic retort from Mom that would poke a withering response out of Dad. Here's where she would say something like, "Great, so we get to look forward to being in the company of a hungry grouch all morning." And then he would say something like, "So? I get to enjoy the company of a grouch *all* the time!"

"Okay," my mother said.

Crystal's eyes widened, as she looked over at me.

Neither of us said a word; we were afraid to break the mood.

What finally moved us out of that idyllic space was an eerie, electric, yet strangely comforting sound, emanating from inside the tent next to us. Crystal heard it first, and she looked up from her Cap'n Crunch and said, "What's that?" With her leading the way, we all four trooped next

163

door to "knock" and to be admitted by our "neighbors," a young couple from New Jersey. There, on their TV, we watched the news of the "Marilyn Miracle," as the reporters were now calling it.

At the moment, the cameras were panning the crowds below the monument, and picking up the noise from down there.

The eerie sound was coming from the crowds.

"Are they chanting?" Mom asked.

"No, listen," the young woman urged us.

And then we could hear that it wasn't *om* the crowds were humming.

It was *MMMMMMM*.

"They say there've been healings," the young woman told us, her eyes as wide as Crystal's had been earlier, when Mom and Dad were courteous to one another. "Sexual healings."

Mom cast a quick glance at Crys and me, and I tried to look bland.

"What's a sexual healing?" my sister blurted out.

Nobody answered her, though I wished somebody would, so I'd know, too! We stayed in their tent long enough (before Mom shooed us out) to get a hint not only of what that meant, but also of what the rest of the world was saying about "us."

"The vision, itself, appears to be a bonafide miracle, accompanied by actual physical miracles," attested one of the people being interviewed. "It is clearly on the order of Fatima or Lourdes, but is even more astonishing and believable, because it has been witnessed, and continues to be seen, by millions of people, if you include those watching it on television." The expert smiled, ever so slightly. "It is certainly not, however, a sighting of the Virgin."

"What's a virgin?" Crys whispered to me.

You, I thought, *and me*. But I put my finger to my lips.

"It's an illusion," claimed a man who was reputed to be an expert in unmasking fraudulent "miracles." "It's a spectacular magic trick to dupe the gullible."

"It is not!" Crystal shouted at his face on the screen. She may not have known what "gullible" meant, but she knew what the man meant. Dad said, "Shh, honey," and pulled her into a hug, and kept her there.

"Heresy," pronounced a high church official. "Blasphemy, for anyone to call this a religious experience!"

From the political right came similar, heated opinions: "It's a national disgrace, having that woman up there with our most beloved and respected presidents!"

But from down below the monument, the interviews were of a different tone, entirely: "She's so beautiful up there," said a man from North Dakota. And a woman from Minnesota was crying, as she said, "I can't stop crying. When I look at her, I can't stop crying, and yet I feel so happy. I can't explain it." And a man from Arizona said, "I loved Monroe in *Some Like It Hot*, and I love Monroe up there, but . . ." He bent down and kissed the forehead of the woman standing beside him, and smiled, as he said, ". . . I love *her* most of all."

"Oh," sighed the young woman from New Jersey. "Isn't that sweet?"

Mom made us leave their tent when medical experts started talking about the normal incidence of cures of impotence in an average population of men, and the statistical likelihood of instantaneous changes in the sexual responses of previously nonorgasmic women.

Down among the "trading posts" and parking lots that

day, we drove into the atmosphere that could only be described as part religious revival, part movie star festival.

Clones of Marilyn (not all of them female, by any means) were arriving by the plane and bus load, accompanied by men dressed up like Tony Curtis, or Jack Lemmon, or Clark Gable, or any one of the male movie stars with whom Marilyn Monroe had appeared in pictures.

People were carrying around little statues of Marilyn, and holding them to their lips, and kissing them. Lots of people were kissing each other, too, which should have been excruciatingly embarrassing, especially for Crystal, but for some reason, it wasn't. As the lady from New Jersey had said, it was sweet. There was a sweetness to that crowd, and a tender courtesy in the way that many men and women were treating one another, a tenderness that only grew as the day progressed from warm to hot by late afternoon.

We heard men saying "please."

And women saying "thank you."

We saw people move back from doorways and murmur, "after you," and we saw shoppers wait patiently in the long lines, and we heard them speak respectfully to waiters and waitresses and sales clerks. We saw people with their arms around each other, and people laughing, and a lot of people crying, for no apparent reason.

As we strolled — carrying our own Marilyn souvenirs — my father held my mother's hand. By afternoon, they each had an arm around the other's waist. Crys and I tagged along all day, unwilling to break away from the feeling of affection that seemed to surround our parents. My sister and I had stopped staring at Marilyn on the mountain by that time; instead we stared at those linked arms, as if *they* were miracles, too.

And that was the third day, when you would have sworn

world peace was at hand, not to mention peace in the war between the sexes.

On the fourth day, all hell broke loose.

For us, it started nearby, right after cereal.

Both the young couple in the tent to the left of us and the family of five in the tent to the right of us had portable televisions, which they seemed to have turned on, watching the news, more than they actually spent down in "town," or even watching the monument. Maybe that's why a fracas broke out between them — because their experience of *her* was so indirect — and wouldn't you know it began as a religious war?

From the tent to the right, we heard a TV preacher inveighing against Marilyn and her image. They had it turned up loud as it would go, clearly hoping all of us heathens would listen, and heed!

"Heed not the Queen of the Realm of Illusion!" shouted the hoarse-voiced preacher. His voice ripped into the tranquility of the morning. "Turn your eyes from the Whore of Babylon! Turn back your eyes to the Queen of Heaven, to God and Our Lord Jesus and His holy Mother! Drop to your knees this instant, and beg God's merciful forgiveness for so much as glancing at this evil image that has arisen steaming from the foul bowels of Hell! God, forgive us who repent, and punish those who persist in their iniquity! Hear us, believe us, that we who are gathered in Thy Name this day, do not love the Harlot! We do not accept the works of the Whore! We plead for the scourge of Thy Fury across the world, to whip the sin from the backs of the lovers of the Harlot! Blind them! So they cannot see her! Deafen them! So they do not hear her! Cripple them! So they bend their knees at last to Thee! Cast the Whore off Thy mountain!

Kill, kill, kill the Harlot, and strike down the wicked who follow her!"

Crystal started looking confused and scared.

"Mom?" she said. "What does that mean?"

Dad was furious, at the noise level, if nothing else.

"I'm going over there and give them a piece of my mind," he fumed, which would once have been Mom's perfect cue to say something like, "That's why you're such a moron! You give so many pieces of your mind away!" But now she only placed both of her hands gently against his chest, and said, "Let's get in the car, and go back to town. Don't you think it might be best to get the girls away from those crazies?"

We were hurrying to do just that, when the couple from New Jersey burst out of their tent and started yelling at the people in the other tent to turn their "damned idiot preacher off!" Which brought out the man from that tent to shake his fist and yell back at them that they were "going straight to hell for worshiping that bitch of Satan!"

It was worse, if possible, in "town."

The forces against the miracle were gathering, even as more "healings" were being reported. Grim-faced people with pamphlets appeared in front of the "trading post." Men carrying large crosses started marching up and down between the cars in the parking lots. Women stood on street corners with their children and yelled Scripture at passersby.

Around lunchtime, there was a rumor that somebody had gone into one of the "trading posts" and had attacked the Marilyn souvenirs with an axe.

Unfortunately, truck after truck of mementos were pouring into the area that day (possibly from those factories in Taiwan Dad had joked about), just as the anti-Marilyn

168

people began arriving in big groups, too. Of course, the sight of all of those bosomy little dolls just fueled the religious and political outrage and determination of some people to "do something about her." We heard several people say, in fact, that they were "going to do something about her."

"What can they do?" Mom wondered, out loud, to us.

"I don't think *they* know," was Dad's opinion.

We, ourselves, actually saw two men shove a man dressed up as Marilyn. The guy in the sequined dress stumbled in his high heels, which caused him to fall against a wall and scrape his bare shoulder. And we heard somebody hiss, "Whore," at a woman who was dressed up to look like Marilyn in the number "Diamonds Are a Girl's Best Friend" from *Gentlemen Prefer Blondes*.

When Mom heard that, she insisted on gathering us up and returning to the campground that minute. When we got there, our neighbors on both sides were quiet, but Dad said to start dismantling our tent, which Crys and Mom and I did, while he went off to try to locate another site for us. I was scared: I didn't want to get hurt, but I didn't want to leave Marilyn, either. I was afraid that if we left Mount Rushmore, our parents might revert to their old ways. The preachers might be screaming about Hell, but the last day and a half had seemed like heaven, to me.

"There's no other space for us here," Dad reported when he returned, and then he looked at all of us, in turn. "Should we go home?"

"No!" Crystal said, and tugged at him. "No! No!"

Dad glanced at me, and I shook my head.

Finally, he took Mom's vote. She didn't say yes or no. Instead, she said, "Let's find a place off by ourselves, in the woods." And that's how we came to move so much closer to *her,* so that we were right where we needed to be in order to become bit players in the final dramatic scene of her last appearance on earth.

By that night, it was — if you'll pardon the pun — crystal clear that somebody was going to have to explain some things to the ten-year-old. Our parents apparently assumed that I'd do the dirty work, as I usually did, but the problem with that convenient theory was that I didn't understand a lot of what was happening any better than Crys did!

It seemed that the healings that hundreds of people were attributing to the apparition were complete cures of an extremely specific sort: All of them were related somehow to sexuality. Some were physical healings of medically confirmed ailments such as ovarian or testicular cancer, while other cures seemed to be more of an emotional or psychological nature. Supposedly, there were men who confessed to having been child molesters, and who now claimed to have no further longings in that direction. In New York City, a convicted rapist was reported to have fallen to his knees in the middle of a prison exercise yard, and to have wept for his victims.

In addition, women who thought they were infertile were finding themselves suddenly pregnant. And women who desperately *didn't* want a baby were discovering their wombs to be mysteriously, blissfully empty! Women who'd always suffered from menstrual cramps were experiencing pain-free periods, and people who had been hiding sexual addictions were publicly declaring themselves liberated from compulsion!

As for me, I just wanted to be hanging around when Mom or Dad explained to Crys the meaning of phrases such as "sustained erection" and "multi-orgasmic"!

Our new campsite was miles closer to Mount Rushmore, close enough so that the lights that illuminated Marilyn and the presidents also cast a soft glow over us.

By suppertime, Crystal's questions were thick as ticks on a leaf.

"Mom, I heard people are getting cured of herpes," Crystal said, over baked beans and hot dogs under the fragrant pines. "What's herpes? I know what AIDS is. Is it true people are getting cured of that, like we heard?"

"I hope so," Mom replied, carefully answering the second question.

"What are genital warts?" Crystal, irrepressibly, asked next.

Dad nearly squirted his hot dog out of its bun, when he heard that.

"Oh, gross!" I blurted, and wished I could disappear.

"Crystal," said my mother, who looked as if she desperately wanted to laugh, "your sister will answer all your questions, after we eat."

"Mom!" I objected, loudly.

"Won't you?" she asked me.

"No! That's your job!"

I didn't want to tell her I didn't have all the answers.

She glanced for help toward Dad, but he only grinned, and said, "Right. That's definitely your job, sweetheart."

"Okay, Crystal," Mom said later, as the two of them sat cuddled together by our campfire. I was right inside the door of our tent, with one ear practically glued to the canvas. Dad had disappeared, on the pretext of gathering firewood. Poor Mom got stuck with the job. I listened for all I was worth, as she stumbled on with her explanations

171

about the facts of life and miracles. "To understand what's going on, you need to understand about Marilyn Monroe."

"She was a movie star," Crys interrupted, in a knowing voice.

"Yes, but a very special one, and there has never been anybody quite like her, either before or since. She was what people call 'sexy.' That meant she was really attractive to the opposite sex — men, I mean — because she was so . . . so . . . uh, well, you know how last year you thought Danny Francis was so cute in your class?"

"Yeah, but Mom, that was last year!"

"I know, honey, but how you felt . . . that, in a great big way, is how millions of men felt about Marilyn Monroe. And not just men. A lot of women thought she was attractive, too. I loved her, for instance. I thought she was kind of embarrassing, because she wore these revealing clothes that made her look practically naked, and she was always flouncing around and wiggling her butt —"

Crystal and Mom giggled, together.

"But even so, I thought she was cute and pretty and funny and adorable." Mom paused, and the campfire filled that quiet moment with the hissing and crackling sounds of its burning. "And now I realize she was also powerful. And intelligent. I can see that in her now, when I look at her old movies. And that power and intelligence, that's all part of being sexy, too. Anyway . . ."

Mom's voice rushed on, before Crys could ask more questions.

"Sex is a powerful feeling of attraction between two people. It's part of what makes people fall in love. It brings people together to have babies. It's perfectly normal. But it can be used in healthy or unhealthy ways. Just like money can, or food, or anything else you can think of. Sex can

172

cause good things to happen to people, or bad things."

Mom's words were coming slower now, as if she was choosing them ever more carefully, or maybe just thinking about what they meant as she said them.

"For some reason that none of us understands, this vision of Marilyn on the mountain is causing good things to happen to people, in regard to sex, and it's also undoing some bad things that have happened to them in regard to sex."

"Why?" Crystal asked.

The fire sang while I, too, waited for Mom's answer.

"Because we needed it, I guess," she said, so softly I barely heard her. "And maybe it had to be her, because she knew what it was like to need — to need so very much — to be healed."

"She?" Crys said.

"Marilyn."

"I love her," Crystal declared.

"I love her, too, honey."

Inside the tent, I thought, *Me, too.*

That was the moment I realized that I didn't hate the vacation or my parents, and that I didn't resent my little sister, not anymore. I felt good, better than I'd ever felt before in my life. I knew what it was like then to feel whole. Complete. Young. Hopeful and happy. *Thank you, Marilyn,* I whispered. I closed my eyes, and pictured her on Mount Rushmore. *Thanks very much.*

By the dawn of the fifth day, many of the people who believed the apparition was an abomination had, with seemingly incredible swiftness, formed themselves into a loud, aggressive coalition.

Dad went into "town" by himself early that morning,

and came back talking of rumors of dynamite, of "blowing her off the mountain," of the National Guard being sent in to disperse the crowds and maintain order, of incidents of violence in the crowds, overnight, and of beatings and arrests, and of people being shipped off to jails wherever there was room to hold them in the little towns of South Dakota. He said he didn't know how much of what he'd heard was true. But Dad said he did know this was no longer a happy place to be, and that if there wasn't trouble now, there soon would be.

"I want to get you and the girls out of here," he told Mom.

But she looked thoughtfully at Crystal and me and then astonished me, at least, by saying, "The girls and I aren't ready to leave." She ordered me to take Crys for a walk in the woods "while your father and I sort this out." But before I could turn away, she said to me, "What's that on your face?"

My left hand flew to an itchy spot on my lower left cheek, where I felt something bumpy and kind of rough, and I immediately thought, *Damnation*, how come other people get cured of cancer, but I still get pimples?

Mom drew me close to her and squinted at the thing.

"It's a mole," she pronounced, and then she drew back from me . . . looked up at Marilyn on the mountain . . . looked back at me . . . looked over at Dad . . . and breathed, "Oh, my God, do you know what this is?"

It was a beauty mark, exactly like *hers*.

Mom called it a stigmata — which she explained was like Christ's wounds appearing in the hands of saints and martyrs. But Dad said she'd better not use that word loosely, especially not in "town," what with all the religious fanatics gathered there, and every one of them just looking for any excuse to be offended, and to strike out against the of-

174

fender, which in this case would be me.

My sister looked at me doubtfully. "A saint?"

I kept touching the beauty mark, until Mom pulled my hand away from it.

"We have to talk," she said to Dad.

As we plodded off together onto our assigned walk in the woods, Crystal muttered, "It's not fair. I want one."

"Maybe when you're older," I told her, smugly.

She thwapped me with the back of her hand, and I laughed, feeling extraordinarily special and pleased with myself.

We stayed, and we even made a brief foray into town that fifth day, though I received stern instructions to keep my head down. Dad wanted to make me wear a head scarf, but Mom said that made me look even more like Marilyn during the period when she was married to the playwright. They compromised by sticking a bandage on my face, which made me feel embarrassed to be seen in public. Protesting did me no good; they said it was for my own safety.

Once in "town," however, we discovered I was not the only one to have received what the agitators were already calling "the mark of Marilyn." Girls and women all up and down the streets, and in the parking lots and "trading posts," were sprouting similar beauty marks, and some of the females wearing them were furious about it, because they were among the agitators. Dad said we were lucky that was the case, because the fact that it was also happening to them was probably the only thing that kept them from actually calling it the "mark of the Beast."

I felt let down, that I wasn't the only one.

People who felt as we did had almost disappeared from

175

the congested area below the monument, because it was getting too dangerous to be there. If you were seen carrying a Marilyn souvenir, or wearing a Marilyn costume, you were accosted by people accusing you of being a traitor to America, or a blasphemer against God, or both, and you stood a risk of having your souvenir jerked out of your hands, or your costume torn off of you, and of being shoved, or worse. People who'd come like pilgrims hoping to be healed were shown on television as they stood weeping in disappointment, some of them, still at the airports in Rapid City and Sioux Falls, afraid to venture any further down the road to Mount Rushmore. At the "trading posts," the merchants swept the Monroe sales items off their shelves and put the presidents back in their front windows.

Mom and Dad hurried us away almost as soon as we arrived, but not before we saw the huge demolition machinery moving into "town," and not before we heard more of the rumors about "pinpoint explosives."

"Why do they hate her?" Crys asked, and asked, and asked. She was hyper with too much energy, bouncing up and down on the back seat of our car and chattering, chattering, chattering, until she drove us all crazy, and we all snapped at her. "Mom? Dad? Why do they hate her? Why do they want to kill her? Why do they call her those names? What's *wrong* with her?"

"Crystal, sit *down*," Dad finally told her.

"And be *quiet* for five minutes!" Mom said, sounding frantic herself.

"Please!" I chimed in.

Of course, Crys burst into tears. Feeling awful and guilty about taking it all out on her, I turned my face to the car window. Out of their sight, I gently rubbed my beauty spot, over and over, with the first two fingers of my right hand.

According to the news bulletins we heard on our car radio, the U.S. government truly was sending in the National Guard to keep order, but nobody seemed to think they could mobilize in time to save Marilyn, not that that was their objective, anyway. Their mission was to maintain law and order, and to protect the presidents.

"How," asked a talk-show deejay sympathetic to the apparition, "can they stop a dedicated cadre of explosives experts, anyway? In that wilderness around the monument? No way! Listen, folks, the bad guys are probably already on their way, armed to the teeth with dynamite, or nitroglycerin, or plastic explosives, or whatever it takes to slice our girl off the mountain. Talk to me, Callers! What's your opinion?"

At our tent, with the Ponderosa pines guarding our privacy like sentinels, we got more and more quiet as the day progressed, even Crystal, who kept breaking into convulsive little bursts of tears, and needing Mom or Dad to give her a hug and stroke her hair and lie to her and tell her it was all going to be all right.

"How can you tell her that?" I whispered, furiously, to Mom.

"Honey," she said, so gently it made me feel even more angry, "it *is* going to be all right. We'll go back home. You'll go back to school. Life will go on as usual. We'll forget all about Marilyn."

I touched my beauty mark. "I'll *never* forget her!"

Mom tried to hug me, but I wouldn't let her. I stalked off a little way into the woods, and my head filled up with the words, *I won't . . . ever . . . forget . . . you!*

At least, we got over making Crys the family scapegoat.

Nobody snapped angrily at her anymore. I came back into camp, my anger spent on hurling pine cones into space, and we just all walked around, or lounged around, like zombies, turning on the car radio every so often, and getting more discouraged and feeling more hopeless as the sun crossed over the monument and slid down the other side of it.

The spotlights came on, illuminating Washington, Jefferson, Lincoln, Roosevelt, and Monroe, for the last time.

The chanting started around 11 P.M.

It floated through the woods to us, winding around the pines, scooting along the ground and carried with the cold breeze of that summer evening. It woke us up, one by one, in our tent, and pulled us by our curiosity out into our little clearing.

"What in the world?" Dad murmured.

Crys and I had slept in our jeans and T-shirts, Mom and Dad had pajamas on, and we were all barefoot and rumple-haired and sleepy. For some reason, Mom ran back into the tent and put on her own jeans and T-shirt and a jacket, and even her socks and hiking boots. She threw jackets out at Crys and me, and then she insisted we both put shoes on.

She didn't say anything to Dad, so he just stood there, listening.

By the time Crys and I got back outside, the chanting was louder, and coming near us.

MMMMMMMMMM

That's all it was, a humming of that letter of the alphabet, and it sounded like a melodious, resonant, high-pitched wave rolling toward us, some of it sung in soprano, some in alto, for it was all women and girls who were chanting, and marching across the plain toward the monu-

178

ment. Within minutes, they reached us, and Mom took one of Crystal's hands and one of mine, and the three of us melted into the pines to become notes in the moving melody.

Dad started to hurry back into the tent to change clothes, but Mom stopped him with a softly voiced, "No, sweetheart." And when he then moved as if he'd join us, pajamas and all, she tugged her hand free from mine, blew him a kiss, and called back to him, "Somebody needs to stay here and guard the fort!"

I caught a glimpse of my father, standing there with the breeze whipping the ankles of his pajamas, and he staring at us, looking so worried, as if he were afraid he'd never see us again.

But he didn't follow us.

We left him behind, and joined the other women, dozens, hundreds of women, and more, all of us merging easily into a cadence with one another with every bold and quiet stride we took, softly humming as we marched along together to the base of the monument.

"Others are coming from above," one of the marchers told us.

From the Black Hills, from the west, she meant.

I looked for the Lakota woman, and thought I glimpsed her once, among the trees.

By morning's light, we were fully assembled: hundreds of women and girls, stationed at the base of Mount Rushmore; hundreds more of us lining the top of the monument, standing at the very edge that overlooked the plains and the "town" below.

Through a telescope or binoculars, or from an airplane or helicopter, anyone who saw us could read the words on the banner that some of the women draped over the apparition of Marilyn's hair.

It said, in big, black letters:

IF YOU DESTROY HER, YOU'LL KILL US!

And that's the sight that greeted not only the valley, but everybody who switched on a morning television news show. And there we remained, successfully defending *her*, all that sixth day and all of the sixth night, while the monument lights illuminated all of us: Presidents, Marilyn, living women and girls. Food materialized from somewhere, and water as we needed it, and somehow there were bedrolls for the children, who organized their own games to play.

No one dared to touch her as long as we remained.

I think we could have stayed, if not indefinitely, then certainly a long, long time, because reinforcements, other women and girls, began arriving by the morning of the seventh day. But as it turned out, we didn't have to stay, because *she* took matters into her own hands.

The word came first to us from observers below.

"They say she's fading!" someone yelled.

We couldn't tell from where we stood and guarded her. We were too close to the image to be able to judge whether it appeared as dark and clear upon the mountain as it had all week.

"She's leaving the mountain!" the word came down.

And she was. Slowly, over the course of the seventh day, she took her leave of us, having drawn out of us our courage and our independence, having been protected by us when we believed she most needed it. Now she freed us by vanishing as mysteriously as she had come.

By the time the lights came on that night, she was gone.

As you know, the Crazy Horse monument was never finished.

Some people thought he'd gone chasing after her. If that's true, I'd call that a *really* Happy Hunting Ground! But I think he had too much dignity for that. Personally, I think she pulled his image away with her as a favor to a great man, knowing he would never have wanted to be there in the first place. How could she do that? Well, you know her magnetic appeal! She didn't take the presidents with her — obviously — and, to me, they look incomplete now, without her voluptuous, vibrant, incandescent femininity to balance them.

However, if you compare photos of them now with pictures of them before *she* appeared, you'll swear there has been a softening of the presidential brows, a loosening of tension in Tom's lips, a twinkle in George's stern glance. Abraham looks as if his load's been lightened, he looks encouraged and comforted, I think, and a little ashamed of himself for hanging up there on the Lakota's sacred mountain. None of those four had very enlightened attitudes toward the native peoples, after all, and Abe was no better than he had to be, in that regard. I know I'm reading a lot into stone, but over time even stone changes, doesn't it? The most dramatic transformation I detect is in Teddy, who used to look as if he were only peering over the plains for the biggest stag to shoot. Now I believe there's a hint of awe and tenderness in his gaze, as if he's deeply moved and even humbled by all he surveys. Any woman who could humble Teddy Roosevelt was a saint, in my book!

Everybody has forgotten, except the rest of the world and me.

Maybe, when she left, she took America's memory with her, because the important thing was not the conscious memory of her apparition, but the unconscious changes she wrought in us. We women are different now — stronger, more straightforward and honest — and so are our men, many of them just plain nicer people than they were before.

So maybe it doesn't really matter if everybody's beauty mark faded, except mine, evidently, or that even Crystal thinks I'm crazy when I try to remind her of our astonishing vacation to the Black Hills when she was ten years old.

It's not that I'm lonely with this memory. After all, I've got the rest of the world to remember it with me. It's just that I'd like her to get the credit, that's all.

So, now, can you see *her* there, on Mount Rushmore?

Are you beginning to remember?